I0650317

Fairfax L. Cartwright

Olga Zanelli

A tale of an imperial city. Vol. 2

Fairfax L. Cartwright

Olga Zanelli
A tale of an imperial city. Vol. 2

ISBN/EAN: 9783337088781

Printed in Europe, USA, Canada, Australia, Japan

Cover: Foto ©Andreas Hilbeck / pixelio.de

More available books at **www.hansebooks.com**

OLGA ZANELLI

OLGA ZANELLI

A Tale of an Imperial City

BY

FAIRFAX L. CARTWRIGHT

" . . . dans cette vie
Rien n'est bon que d'aimer n'est vrai que de souffrir "

VOLUME   SECOND

LONDON

SWAN SONNENSCHEIN & CO

PATERNOSTER SQUARE

OLGA ZANELLI.

CHAPTER XVII.

IT was about the middle of summer, and as Berlin at that season of the year is intolerably hot and disagreeable Count Klinkenstein had hired a small villa at Potsdam for his mistress. It was a pretty little house built on a slight elevation above the lake, and having a quaint old-fashioned garden which ran down to the water's edge. Lolo's many friends did not forget her in her rural retreat, and they would often come to spend the hot afternoons in the months of July and August in her pleasant garden. Baron Zerbino, however, was not of the number, for he had been removed from the Italian Embassy in Berlin to another post, and although Count Klinkenstein was very fond of him he did not miss his friend as much as he would have done a year before, for now he had a mistress in whose society he passed most of his time. When the nights were warm and the moon was shining, making the great girdle of pine forest look weird and fantastic in the dim light, Lolo would organise, what she liked best, a water-party ; then entering the pretty boat the Count had given her, and followed by a large crowd of others all hung with Chinese lanterns, she would begin singing Italian songs accompanying herself on the guitar, and in the stillness of the night her voice would be borne over the water to many a distant villa on the borders of the lake, and the staid and solemn wives of privy councillors of various degrees would remark to their husbands, with an air of pious horror, that the brazen-faced wench was again indulging in an orgy. Lolo, it must be acknowledged, was well known in the neighbourhood, and even had she been the most chaste of saints, the luxury she lived in, her good looks, and that peculiar power she possessed of fascinating the men who came into contact with her, would still have exposed her to the calumnies and envy of her sex.

"What will you do, Edward ?" said Lolo one evening to Count Klinkenstein as they sat together in an arbour in their garden.

"I do not quite know," he replied ; "but I suppose I will have to go and stay with my uncle. He is very imperative in his letter ; I do not think that I can refuse. You see he was my guardian once, and he still thinks he has a right to be obeyed." Then he pulled out Count Eckstein's letter and read it over again.

"You will not be away very long, Edward, will you ?" she replied, leaning her head against his shoulder. "As yet we have not been parted from each other even for a single day ; I do not know how I shall bear it if you go. I shall live in seclusion and close my doors to all visitors. I will say to any one who calls that I am ill and cannot receive him. It will be true, you see, for I am sure to be out of sorts while you are away. How many days does your cruel uncle propose to keep you ? "

" A week, Lolo ; and he even hints that he would like me to stay longer."

" A whole week ! Do not stay away so long, Edward ; you know I want you to be near me just now."

" But, my darling Lolo, I shall be no great distance off, and moreover we can talk to each other by telegraph all day long. I shall also take with me the large new photograph of yourself, so that I shall always have you before my eyes ; however, I shall take care not to let my uncle see it."

" Do you think he would be very angry if he knew of my existence ? "

" Well, Lolo, I am afraid he might make some disagreeable remarks which would rouse my anger, and I might then do something foolish. If he spoke irreverently about you, I am quite capable of knocking him down."

" And then he would turn you out of the house, and you would return to me the sooner," she said, laughing.

" It might be more serious than you think, Lolo, for the Prussian military law considers it a grave offence for a lieutenant to knock down a general, even if he is his uncle ; were it not so there would be no stability in the army."

"What does your uncle want you for?"

"I have no idea, Lolo."

"I am sure, Edward, that if he has anything to say he can do it in less than a week. Do you not think you might suggest to him that he should come up to Berlin to see you instead of your going down to him?"

"It would never do, Lolo; you seem to forget that he is a general, and that it is not proper for me to argue with him."

"What a great man a general must be, Edward, if he can command so much respect and obedience from a nephew!"

"Now do not be silly, Lolo; you know perfectly well that I would prefer to stay here; I cannot, however, help myself. When I return to Berlin I will immediately apply for a week's leave of absence and get this visit over as quickly as possible. It must be done; moreover, my sister is staying with my uncle, and I have not seen her for a very long time."

"You have got a sister, Edward?" exclaimed Lolo, turning round and looking at him with astonishment; "why did you never tell me so before?"

"I did not think that it would interest you," he replied, rather annoyed, and feeling somewhat ashamed of himself for having mentioned the existence of his sister to his mistress.

"Everything which relates to you interests me," she said in her winning way, putting her arm round his neck; "tell me all about her. I know I can never see her, so I must form my picture of her from what you tell me. Won't you speak? Are you annoyed at my asking these questions?"

He gave her a kiss, and replied: "Lolo, let us talk of other subjects."

She was ever ready to do anything to please him, so she made no further allusions to his journey. After dinner they sat on the balcony of the villa, and gradually the conversation began to flag, and they both fell into a state of reverie as they watched the moon rising slowly over the low hills covered with pine forest, and saw the first rays beginning to be reflected in the still waters of the lake. They were brought back to the realities of this world by a servant announcing that the Count's carriage was waiting at the door to take him to the station.

"I suppose I must be off, Lolo; if they grant me my leave I shall be to-morrow night at my uncle's country house, boring myself exceedingly and thinking of you all the time. How I shall long for the end of the week, when I will be able to rush back to you, and kiss you and hold you again in my arms as I am doing now! I shall have to put on a solemn face and behave properly all the time I am down there, for I can assure you, Lolo, my uncle's house is not a pleasant one to spend a week in; he is a serious man, and not at all given to frivolity. What a nuisance to be sure it is to have uncles and cousins."

"You have got a cousin, Edward?"

"Yes, Lolo."

"A female cousin?"

"Yes."

"How old is she?"

"I really do not know, Lolo; but I suppose somewhere about eighteen."

"Edward!" cried Lolo, starting up, "you are hiding the truth from me; your uncle has sent for you, because he wants you to marry her."

"You are quite mad, Lolo," replied Count Klinkenstein; "who could expect me to marry at my age! The idea has never entered into my head, and I am certain my uncle has other things to think about than to select a wife for me. Besides, I hardly know my cousin. I have not seen her since she was quite a small girl, and it is not usual for people to marry before they have seen each other. Do not be so foolishly alarmed, Lolo; I have told you over and over again that I had no intention of ever getting married." Then he continued to soothe and pacify her until the servant appeared again and informed him that unless he started at once he would miss his train. Lolo accompanied Count Klinkenstein to the door, and as the carriage drove away, and he waved to her a last farewell, she could not help being seized with a vague feeling of apprehension that this journey to the country boded her no good.

The next day Count Klinkenstein applied to the authorities for a week's leave of absence, and having obtained it he started for Count Eckstein's country seat in Pomerania. It was not without a certain amount of misgivings that he began his journey, for he was well aware that on nearly every occasion on which his uncle had sent for him it had been either to give him a lecture or to ply him with good advice, which Count Klinkenstein considered quite unneces- sary, and a sign of superfluous affection on the part of an uncle for his nephew. However, on this occasion he expected rather a lecture, and a severe one, than a dose of good advice, for he could not close his eyes to the fact that his liaison with Olga Zanelli was perfectly well known to all his brother officers in Berlin, and that it would be very extraordinary if his uncle had not heard of it. As the train rattled along he fell into meditations, and turned over in his mind what answer he should return to his uncle if questioned on this delicate subject; he came to the conclusion that it would be best to avoid the subject as long as possible, but he was resolved that if he were forced into giving an answer he would inform his respected uncle that it was out of the question for him to give up Olga Zanelli.

Count Klinkenstein did not feel in the best of humours as the train pulled up at the little country station where he had to get out. A carriage was wait- ing for him, which he entered at once, and after a short drive he found himself within his uncle's domains. The ancestral home of the Ecksteins was not remark- able for architectural beauty; the buildings were low and squat, and their uninteresting appearance was not redeemed by picturesque scenery, for the country was flat, studded here and there with woods of birch and pine. Surrounding the house was a kind of park, but no wall separated it from the ploughed land beyond and the not far distant village.

Count Eckstein was standing at the doorway of his house as his nephew drove up.

"I am very glad to see you have come, Edward," he said, shaking him warmly by the hand; "very glad indeed, for I have seen so little of you of late. I hope you will stay some time with us: your sister is anxiously waiting to see you, and so is Nelly ; go upstairs, my boy, you will find them all there."

Count Klinkenstein did as he was bid, and left the old General to begin his usual afternoon inspection of his garden and his hot-houses. He was a fine old man was Count Eckstein, erect, with a thin, close-shaven face and iron-grey hair. He was an honour-able and straightforward gentleman, with a strong sense of duty, and to him duty meant implicit obedience to his Emperor. As might be expected his principles were those of an ultra-Conservative, and the only newspaper he allowed in his house was the *Gazette of the Cross*. Proud of his ancestry, many of whom had acquired renown in the career of arms, with a blind faith in the high duties encumbent on the nobility, Count Eckstein was nevertheless the most courteous of men, and always kind and affable to his servants and dependents. In religion he was a stern Puritan, and he never would condescend to argue with any one who took up the defence of the Roman Catholic religion : it had wandered away from the true path of the Christian doctrine ; he had conclusively made up his mind upon that point ; then why engage in irritating controversies ? Besides, had not the Protestant house of Hohenzollern restored the unity of Germany and re-established the empire? Could there be a better proof that Heaven was on her side? He never allowed a day to pass without reading a chapter or two from the Bible, which lay ever by his side on his writing-table, and on Sundays the household was drawn up two and two and marched to the little village church by the General in person. It was said of him that at the battle of Königgrätz, when he was shot in the leg while leading his regiment to the attack, he had sat down by the wayside, and to encourage his men had begun to chant one of Martin Luther's spirited hymns with all the gravity of a cathedral chorister.

Count Klinkenstein met with a warm reception from his sister, whom he had not seen for more than a year; and his bright and good-humoured cousin Nelly, the spoilt daughter of the old General, fell round his neck, German fashion, and kissed him repeatedly.

Nelly had certainly grown very pretty since Count Klinkenstein had last seen her, and as she conducted him over the premises to show him her tame fawn and rabbits, her poultry and other domestic pets, he, following in a pensive mood, thinking of Lolo, came to the conclusion that were it not for his liaison he might do worse than allow himself to fall in love with his pretty cousin.

"Edward, are you fond of Berlin?" asked Nelly, one morning, as she leant languidly against the palings of the paddock, and called her fawn to eat bread out of her hands.

"Of course I am," he replied, waking from a

reverie, for he was generally occupied in thinking about his mistress.

"I do so want to go there, Edward, but my father says I must wait till next winter, when he will present me at court, and then we are to live in Berlin during the season and your sister is to take me out into society. There are lots of museums and interesting things to see in Berlin, are there not?"

"I believe there are some museums, Nelly; but I have never been inside them."

"Are you so occupied when you are in Berlin, Edward?"

"Well, we officers have a good deal to do, Nelly. You see we are expected to get up very early to drill our men."

"But that does not occupy the whole day, does it?"

"We have a great many other occupations."

"Amusing occupations," she replied, laughing. "You do not look overworked."

"Of course, Nelly, we have some amusements, without them life would be too monotonous. You would not like us to spend our whole day with our loutish soldiers?"

"No, not quite; but my father says that nowadays the young officers of the Guard do nothing but amuse themselves, and that they spend a great deal of money which they did not do in the old days when he was a young officer."

"I am sure your father is mistaken," replied Count Klinkenstein, hurriedly, for he was half afraid that his uncle might have dropped some observations about his extravagant expenditure on Lolo, and that Nelly might have heard them.

"But tell me, Edward, what do you do to amuse yourselves in Berlin?" said Nelly, after a short pause.

"Oh! there are theatres and ballets at the Opera, and plenty of balls in the winter, and suppers,—I did not quite mean that,—and a very good circus, and many other things."

"I do so wish to go to a theatre, but I am afraid my father will not let me, for whenever I have asked him to take me to one he has always answered that I was too young for such things."

"That is all nonsense; I will take you, Nelly."

"And shall we go and see Schiller's pieces acted, Edward? I have read most of them, and learnt long passages out of them by heart."

"Of course, if you want to see them, Nelly, you can do so; but nobody nowadays goes to see them; they are so very dull."

"Do you think so? But if they are so dull and nobody goes to see them why do they act them?"

"I did not mean, Nelly, that actually nobody went to see them; I meant that nobody in society went there; schoolgirls are taken to see them for educational purposes."

"Then what are the fashionable pieces to see, Edward?"

"Oh! if you want to be amused you will have to go and hear Offenbach's things and similar productions."

"They are musical compositions, are they not?"

"Yes, and most delightful ones too. I will take

you to see *La Belle Hélène* and *La Vie Parisienne*,
and similar works by other composers, such as *La
Mascotte* and *Gillette de Narbonne.* They are very
exhilarating when you feel dull."

"But, Edward, are not all these pieces French?"

"Yes; but what is the harm of that?"

"Oh! I am afraid my father will not allow me to
go and see them then, for I know he has a strong
dislike of everything French."

"Then I must say, Nelly, your father is very silly."

"Edward! how can you say such a thing?"

"I did not quite mean that, Nelly;—I meant that
he was rather antiquated in his ideas. It is a remnant
of those prejudices which date from the days of Jena
when Napoleon paid us a visit in Berlin. Your father
must have inherited these views from his father, who
fought against Napoleon; but, Nelly, I assure you, that
now everything which is sprightly and amusing comes
from Paris, and there is no harm in laughing and
being amused, is there?"

The Countess Nelly replied nothing for a few minutes,
but continued to feed her fawn.

"Edward," she said after a bit, "are there no other
amusements in Berlin but theatres?"

"If you care about dancing, Nelly, you can have any
amount of it, as at every ball there are at least ten
young officers who dance to every lady present."

"That must be very delightful."

"No doubt it is, Nelly; for any amount of flirting
goes on, and girls when they are pretty get married
very quickly in Berlin."

Nelly blushed and did not answer.

" You do not object to that, do you, Nelly ? " inquired her cousin.

" What a question to ask ! " she said, turning her face away. Then a pause followed, during which Count Klinkenstein looked abashed, and to hide his confusion began with great eagerness to feed the ducks which were waddling and quacking between the legs of the pet fawn.

" Edward," began Nelly again, " do you know that my brother is to join a cavalry regiment at Berlin in a year or so ? "

" Indeed ! then I suppose you will settle down in Berlin for good ? "

" I think it is probable that we shall be there the greater part of the year when my brother enters the Guards. Are you not pleased, Edward ? "

Count Klinkenstein was not at all pleased at the idea, for he felt that the continual presence of his uncle and his pretty cousin in Berlin would be a bore to him now that every one in society was well aware of his relations with Olga Zanelli.

" Nelly, do you really think you will like Berlin ? If I were you I would only go there for the few weeks in the winter during which the court balls take place. You see you are accustomed to a country life ; you will never care for a town life now ; you will miss your garden, your trees, your flowers, and your pet animals. I am sure you will not care about the society ; it is so small, so given to talking scandal, so narrow-minded in its ideas ; in fact, so very provincial."

" But I thought Berlin was such a large city."

"So it is, Nelly; there are heaps of inhabitants in it, but the society you will be introduced to is very exclusive and limited in numbers. Of course there are many young officers, as I said before, but they have not got many ideas beyond dancing and looking smart."

"How strange! Edward, what becomes of all the other people? They cannot all be uneducated and poor."

"Oh dear, no! they are not at all uneducated, and many of them are very well off; but still, you see they do not belong to the same society as ourselves, so we do not see them."

"Why is that?"

"I suppose it is because the chamberlains say that they cannot be invited to court, whereas we can be."

"Oh! I see; but still there ought to be a great many rich men in Berlin, and if a man is rich he ought to be educated and respectable."

"We do not think so in Germany, Nelly; there are, of course, plenty of rich people in Berlin, but they are mostly Jews, and we never speak to a Jew unless he is very rich indeed."

"That is very strange, Edward. Why should there be so many Jews in Berlin while we have none in the country?"

"I cannot explain it, Nelly, unless it be that like in the Old Testament the Jews still travel about and settle down in tribes."

The approach of Count Eckstein put an end to the conversation.

"I would like to speak to you, Edward," said the General to his nephew, who was about to follow his pretty cousin who, having finished feeding her pets, was returning to the house with an empty basket under her arm.

There was nothing left to do but to obey, and Count Klinkenstein resigned himself to listen to a homily from his uncle.

" Edward," began Count Eckstein, with a considerable amount of solemnity, " I want to speak to you seriously. Your father when he died recommended you to my care, and I therefore consider it my duty to give you advice when I see that you are going wrong. Now, my dear boy, I do not wish to pry into your private life, and I assure you that I have not gone out of my way to discover what sort of a life you have been leading in Berlin. What I have heard about you has been from old friends who thought it right that I should know what you were doing. I am afraid, Edward, that you are leading a very fast life ; it is confirmed to me from all sides. It seems that although you have been but a very short time in Berlin you have already borrowed largely. Surely your income was large enough to have satisfied every reasonable desire ! They tell me you gamble largely, and that you spend much money upon women. Now, my dear Edward, I do not wish to be harsh upon you ; I know full well to what temptations a young officer of the Guards is exposed to, and that young men will be young men ; gambling is bad enough, and may reduce you to poverty, but women, Edward, will ruin you body and soul ; and of all the dangers to which a young man in your position is exposed none is greater than to begin a liaison with a woman from which he is afterwards unable to free himself. Now, my dear Edward, there are special reasons why you should not ruin yourself by dissipation and fast living. You are not an ordinary person ;—you are the bearer of a great name ;—you have responsibilities and duties to fulfil ;—you are an officer in the Guards ;— you have to serve your country and your king, and not to satisfy your passions and inclinations. The stability of the empire rests on the virility and moral worth of our German nobility. I regret to see a tendency in our young officers, developing with amazing rapidity, to indulge in luxury and dissipation. I am alarmed at it, for I foresee that it may lead to a catastrophe. Society is disintegrating ; the lower classes are pressing forwards ; the upper classes who ought to be the guides of the nation are growing effete. By hard labour, by simplicity of life and strict economy, by steady perseverance, the empire has been built up. What we have achieved it is our duty, and especially the duty of our nobility, to maintain. I do not deny that our officers may still be brave—that is the last quality which an aristocracy loses ; so were the French officers under the empire, and yet because they had no moral worth France was crushed and Napoleon and his empire disappeared. Let us beware that the same fate does not befall us. We are not born noblemen merely to enjoy certain social advantages or to amuse ourselves ; we have a call and duties to perform ; let us not shirk them ; let us inscribe upon our banner, ' Faith in God ; faith in our Emperor ; faith in our- selves.' "

The old General continued talking in this strain for some time. Count Klinkenstein did not very much relish his uncle's exhortation; he defended himself best he could against the accusations which were heaped upon him; he argued that his uncle had been misinformed; that his expenses were moderate, and that he was leading a very quiet life compared to that led by other young officers. As soon as he could he escaped from the General to enjoy the less stern and more genial society of his sister and his cousin Nelly.

During his stay at Count Eckstein's country seat the Countess Gisèle pressed upon her brother the necessity of his soon thinking about getting married; she wanted to see him settle down and have children, for if he died without an heir the direct line of the house of Klinkenstein would expire. All exhortations to get married were met by Count Klinkenstein with stubborn resistance; he was, he said, too young, too inconstant in his affections, not at all made for married life. The idea of his marrying while his faith was plighted to Olga Zanelli seemed to him too ludicrous for discussion; but he could not tell his sister so, and therefore he did his best to turn the conversation whenever she recurred to that subject.

Count Klinkenstein had been but four days in the country when, on rising from dinner one evening, the servant handed him a telegram. He knew too well from whom it came. He opened it with alacrity and read: "The child is born. It is a girl. Do come back to me as soon as you can. Your ever loving Lolo."

Without saying a word to any one he went out into the garden and began walking up and down in a state of delightful exultation ; he was the father of a child, and its mother was the girl he loved. He was delighted that the event had occurred, for at times he felt misgivings as to whether his love for Lolo would last for ever ; now there could be no question of giving her up, and even his uncle could not ask him to do so. He must remain faithful to the mother of his child. He retired to his bedroom, and sat for some time contemplating Lolo's photograph. All the souvenirs of their common life came back to him : the first meeting at the Magdeburg Station ; her Italian songs which had first touched him ; his courtship ; the fatal evening in the Thiergarten, and then all that had occurred since that date. He kissed her photograph over and over again, and tears came to his eyes as he blamed himself for having deserted her in this moment of trial. He took a pen and wrote a note to his uncle explaining that some urgent business recalled him to Berlin, and early the next morning before the household was stirring he was on his way to town with his heart full of joy and longing to hold Lolo in his arms and to kiss the mother of his child.

CHAPTER XVIII.

IT was midday before Count Klinkenstein drove up to the door of Lolo's villa at Potsdam. In a moment he had made his way upstairs and was by her side. They did not talk much during the first few minutes, but remained silent, looking at each other in the intervals between their kisses. Then Lolo leant over to the cradle by her bedside, and took out her one-day-old child and placed it in Count Klinkenstein's arms. Strange thoughts and feelings passed through him as he fondled his little girl and realised that he was a father. He kissed the babe and played with her till she began to cry, then the nurse had to be summoned to put the infant back into the cradle and to rock it to sleep.

It was a warm summer's day, and Lolo's bed had been drawn near to the open window, so that she could look out upon the garden and the lake and the fir forest beyond.

"Edward, how did you like your visit to the country?" she said to him. "Was your uncle very severe to you as you expected?"

"He did lecture me a good deal, Lolo. He advised me not to enter into a liaison with a woman; that it was very easy to begin and very difficult to break off such engagements, and that to live with a woman who is not your wife generally led a man to perdition. I listened deferentially to the old General just as a student listens to the dull lecture of some professor; but all the while, Lolo, I was thinking of you, and how useless it was to try and make me give you up."

"Are you really speaking the truth, Edward? How about your cousin whose name I have forgotten?"

"My cousin Nelly? She is a very nice girl, much prettier than I had expected; but what has she got to do with you, Lolo? She is not your rival in any way."

"Edward, tell me truly, did they not give you to understand that they wished you to marry her?"

"My sister did suggest it to me rather strongly, but I told her that the idea that I should get married was too ludicrous to be discussed seriously, and I begged her not to irritate me by harping upon the subject."

"But why is it ridiculous, Edward?"

"Because, Lolo, there is that child in the cradle, which will prevent my ever being separated from you."

Lolo though weak raised herself on her pillows, and soon he felt her arms cast round his neck and her dishevelled hair playing about his face as her burning lips touched his forehead.

Count Klinkenstein's duties kept him part of the day in Berlin, but as soon as he was able he would

return to the villa at Potsdam. As for several weeks
Lolo was too weak to receive any visitors, she and
Count Klinkenstein were thrown together a great deal
more than they had ever been before, and the quiet
and more intimate life which they now led seemed
to intensify their affection for each other. The first
day Lolo was able to rise from her bed she sat on the
balcony reclining in a comfortable arm-chair waiting
impatiently for the arrival of her lover. Count
Klinkenstein was rather later than usual on that day.
When he came he was delighted to find her up and
looking so well. Approaching from behind he bent
over her, and as he kissed her wavy hair he
dropped into her lap a pretty casket covered with
blue velvet.

"It is a present I have brought you, Lolo," he said ;
" keep it as a souvenir of your first child."

She opened it, and found a jewel of great price, a
pendant of rubies and diamonds.

"I have selected rubies, Lolo, because their fiery
colour best denotes the ardour of my love."

He took a stool, and sitting by her side, he
received as his reward many a kiss from his loving
mistress.

"It will be my favourite jewel," she exclaimed,
holding it up, and letting the gems sparkle in the
sunlight ; "I shall wear it as often as possible, and
when our little girl is grown up I will give it to
her."

We are so given to making plans for the future.
Little did Lolo know that Count Klinkenstein had
already borrowed largely, and that on that very

morning, with his usual levity in money matters, he had signed a bill on very disadvantageous terms, because he had found that his balance at his bankers was getting very low, and that there was no prospect of any rents coming in from his estates for some time.

"How pretty you look, Lolo," he said, looking up from the low footstool, on which he was seated. "You are getting back all your old colour; but why are you so pensive to-day? You are not usually given to melancholy, are you, Lolo?"

"No, dear," she replied; "I suppose it is because I have been left so long alone this morning, that I have allowed myself to indulge in dreams."

"And what were they about?"

"There is only one subject which interests me, Edward, and that is love."

"Oh! you were dreaming of love, Lolo? What did your dream tell you? Was it more pleasant than the reality?"

"I was not actually dreaming, Edward: I was merely thinking what a curious thing love was. What is it which makes two people suddenly feel such an attraction for each other, and what is it which makes them cling together through life?"

Count Klinkenstein was in good humour that day, and not at all inclined to enter into metaphysical speculations.

"My darling Lolo, what is the use of worrying ourselves as to what may be the nature of love; we possess the article, you will not deny that, I hope. Is that not enough? But if you particularly wish to know what it is which attracts me to you I will tell you, Lolo ; it is your pretty face."

" But that will not last for ever."

" Don't talk nonsense, Lolo, you are pretty now ; what does it matter what you will look like years hence, when we shall be both rheumatic and decrepit, and indifferent to each other's looks ; and whoever tells you that we shall be alive then ? You are pretty now, and that is quite enough for me. What more should I want ?"

" You men are all like that ; a pretty face is all you want ; you do not feel so deeply as we women do. If the woman you loved were to die you would form another attachment and forget her ; but I think that when a woman has really loved, her feelings have been stirred to such a depth, and the personality of her lover has been so impressed upon her, that even should she form a new attachment the new lover will be to her but like the effigy of the old one, and his face will assume for her the features of the one she has so often kissed and known so well. You men have no religion in your love ; for you it is but a fancy, and—alas ! very often merely a passing fancy."

" Well, Lolo, it is not nice of you to come and talk to me like that. I thought my love for you was of the purest, most constant, and most noble kind. How can you talk of it in that crude way, as if it were merely a passing fancy ? I am ashamed of you, Lolo." Then the Count, laughing, took her hand and kissed it.

" I see, Edward, you are in a humour to-day to

turn everything into ridicule, so I will not ask you to discuss with me so sacred a subject as love, or to give me a definition of the word, and your views about it."

"You are very wise, Lolo, not to press me to give you a definition of the meaning of the word love. I was never a good hand at guessing conundrums, and seeing that the philosophers have been for ages trying to understand the subject, and have not yet been able to explain it satisfactorily, how could you reasonably expect me to succeed where they have failed?"

"Edward, I did not want to know what the philosophers may have written upon the subject of love; I want to know what are your views."

"My views on love, Lolo? I really think the birth of your child has made you forget a great deal. My views! Well, I should say that they were in full accord with those of the only sensible philosopher I ever came across in my studies; I forget his name, but he was a Frenchman, and he understood love, for he defined it as, 'L'échange de deux fantaisies et le contact de deux épidermes.'"

"Oh, bother the philosophers!" answered Lolo. What can they know of love? They want to explain it without understanding it."

"You have hit the right nail on the head, Lolo. How could a dried-up old philosopher understand love? It is ridiculous to try and vivisect love, as if it were an animal—a tangible thing. The only philosophers who understand love are persons like ourselves who are young, and we cannot define it, nor do I think that we lose much by not being able to do so. Let us leave love to look after itself. I am sure Cupid knows his business much better than we do, and we shall only irritate him if we try to give him directions. Let us talk about some other subject, Lolo."

"By all means," she replied. "There is another subject of conversation always at hand."

"I hope it is an interesting one."

"Yes, Edward ; we will talk about the child."

"Good heavens, Lolo, you are an odd creature. Is there nothing else for us to talk about but the child ? Look at her ; she is perfectly quiet and gentle, not crying for anything, and very sensibly fast asleep in her cradle. As she is so unobtrusive, and not calling attention to herself, pray let us leave her alone !"

"Edward, you have the language and the ideas of the barrack-room to-day. The child ought to be a delightful subject of conversation to you ; she is a dear little girl, and I hope that when she grows up she will have more sentiment in her than her father."

"How can you say, Lolo, that I have got no sentiment in me ? I am full of sentiment ; and as for the child, she will become an infinitely more interesting subject of conversation when she is grown a little older."

"But there is no reason, Edward, why we should not let our imagination forestall the future. Just imagine what endless subjects for conversation we would have, if we would discuss together the little

girl's future, and picture to ourselves her life
from now to the time when she shall be grown
up."

"Time, Lolo, seems to me to go by quite fast
enough without our exerting ourselves to forestall
it. Besides, what would be the use or satisfaction
of picturing to ourselves a brilliant future for the
little girl, who as yet has not even got a name,
or to delude ourselves with hopes that she may
turn out a success? The future will resent any
attempt on our part to guess what is in store for
us ; and if you do not take care we shall be punished
by finding some day that the child has turned
out a failure and become an exceedingly naughty
girl."

"Do not talk like that, Edward, or you will really
make me very angry ; how can you suggest for a
moment that she would turn out naughty !"

"Well, Lolo, we will not quarrel about her ; my only
wish is that she may turn out as pretty as her
mother, then I will willingly forgive her any naughti-
ness on her part."

Lolo did not answer anything, but lay back in
her arm-chair. She was still weak and pale, but
her pallor became her. Count Klinkenstein, seated
on his footstool, was leaning his head against her
knees ; he passed her arm round his neck, and
touched her hand with his lips.

"It is foolish for us to quarrel, Lolo, is it not?
especially about the child. Lolo !" and he drew
her arm closer round his neck, " I think that we are
both so constituted that a too long abstinence from

love embraces tends to make our humours disagreeable." He raised himself and, kneeling on the footstool, passed his arms round her waist and pressed his forehead against her bosom. "Lolo," he whispered, "I have known you as a girl, let me now know you as a mother."

His words brought back to her mind souvenirs of that night when, after having met her in the Thiergarten, he had brought her home to his rooms ; she remembered how he had lain at her feet on that occasion and poured out in passionate words his love for her. She took his head in her hands, and, bending down slightly to meet his lips, placed on them a long and loving kiss.

So let us leave them.

By the end of September Lolo was in high spirits and back in her pretty apartment in Berlin. She met with an enthusiastic reception from all her acquaintances and friends, and the old and elegant French Duke assured her in his bad German that she had put away the graces of girlhood to become one of the most beautiful women he had ever known in his long career as critic of ladies' charms. Lolo's life now became a wild round of amusements, and Count Klinkenstein, who began to feel the need of continual excitement, encouraged her in every way to entertain company and to amuse herself. Since the preceding year the number of her acquaintances had increased very largely, and she was now on speaking terms with most of the young officers of the Guard, as well as with many of the older ones who were fathers of families

and who were supposed to be leading quiet and respectable lives. Dinners, suppers, and parties to go
to the play succeeded each other night after night, and
even the discreet Berlin press occasionally contained
little paragraphs about Lolo's doings, and inferred
from them with much satisfaction that the "Welt-
stadt" would soon re-place Paris as the centre for all
the gaieties and elegancies of fashionable life. Yet in
spite of all the stir which went on continually around
her, and the temptations to which she was exposed,
Lolo kept her good name in the midst of a society
which would only have been too ready to report that
she was no more faithful than other men's mistresses,
and no man who knew her had ever seriously said
that he believed that she was faithless to Count
Klinkenstein.

One evening as Count Immersdorf, who had become
one of Lolo's most ardent admirers, was leaving her
house in very bad humour, accompanied by the French
Duke, he remarked,—

"It makes me mad to see a pretty woman like Lolo
in love with that young ass Count Klinkenstein.
What has he done to infatuate her so? I have tried
my best, and I see that nothing will come of it. I
shall give up frequenting her house ; I do not see why
a gentleman of good birth should continue to associate
with Bohemians, Jews, and strolling players, if nothing
is to be gained thereby."

"My dear fellow," replied the Duke, with a certain
cynical tone in his voice, "you are too particular ; if
you want to succeed in love affairs you must give up

your exclusive and aristocratic ideas, for there is
nothing so democratic and equalising as woman's love.
It has been historically proved beyond question of a
doubt that a beautiful woman will pass from the
embrace of a duke into the arms of a groom without
scruple, and apparently without any conception of the
incongruity of her behaviour."

It was a dull, wet morning in November when
Heinrich Lazarus rang the bell at Olga Zanelli's
house. He was always very shy of visiting her, for
he was afraid of meeting the swell persons who
frequented his pretty cousin's rooms, and he wished
to avoid as much as possible increasing the pangs of
hopeless love he felt for her. He had not seen her
since the child was born.

When the servant opened the door Heinrich asked
timidly whether he could see the lady, as he called
her. The servant who knew him shouted to the maid
that it was only the poor cousin, and after he had been
kept waiting a few moments Heinrich Lazarus was
ushered into Lolo's boudoir.

Lolo was lying on a couch in an elaborate dressing-
gown, reading the last number of *La Vie Parisienne*,
and trying to recover from the exhausting fatigues of
a supper-party which had lasted till the early hours
of the morning.

"It is wicked of you, Heinrich, not to have called
before!" she exclaimed, as he entered the room. "You
never came to congratulate me on the birth of my
child.. I suppose you do not even know that I am
a mother?"

In a confused manner he muttered some excuses,
and not knowing quite what to do he went up to her
and kissed her hand with the awkward grace of a
super on the stage. Poor fellow! he knew no better;
nor had he ever seen such delicate salutations offered
to a lady except on the stage. He would no doubt
have preferred to have kissed his cousin as he had
been accustomed to do when a boy, but now she
seemed so great a lady that he was afraid to venture
upon such familiarities.

She burst out laughing, and in tossing her feet off
the couch so as to make room for him to sit by her
side she exposed for a moment a cloud of white
petticoats edged with lace. The momentary sight of
all this luxury sent a blush to Heinrich's face. It
seemed to him that he was dreaming; it was so
difficult to realise that the dainty creature lying on
the couch in the elaborate dressing-gown, with her
costly lace and jewelled rings, was the Lolo he had
known in the woollen stockings.

"How melancholy you look, Heinrich," she said;
"you used not to be like that in the old days. I
suppose it is the horrid theology your father—my
respected uncle—makes you study which puts all
these sour looks into your face?"

"I have given up theology," he replied, with a sigh,
which one might have thought indicated relief at the
idea.

"Really, Heinrich? You are not going to become
a parson? I am so pleased, for they are as a rule
such disagreeable persons."

"I have quarrelled with my father on the subject;

I told him I had no taste for the profession ; he replied that the duty of a son was to obey his father, and to comply with his wishes, and not to come and argue with him as to his tastes. He gave me a long lecture, the gist of which was that a father was the best judge of what was good for his children. I did not answer him that day, but thought the matter over for some time, then, having decisively made up my mind that I would not become a parson, I went and informed my father of the fact."

"And what did he reply, Heinrich ? I can imagine what a scene he must have made."

"He simply told me to go to hell, Lolo."

"What ! in that crude way ? "

"Well, he did not quite use those words, for he quoted a text from the Bible, but the meaning it conveyed was just that."

"Then what are you doing now, Heinrich ? "

"I am serving in a fashionable bookseller's shop in the Unter den Linden. I have a good deal of time to myself, and there are plenty of books on the shelves to read when one has a spare moment. My father, of course, does not speak to me any more, as he considers it ignominious that the son of a court chaplain should serve in a shop."

"I pity you," she said, looking at him ; "I know too well that life behind the counter is not pleasant. How I hated being in that milliner's shop ! I was so glad to get away from it."

"And you are happy now, Lolo ? "

"Certainly ; what should I complain of ? Have I

not told you that I am in love? A woman is never really unhappy when she is in that state."

" How different women must be from us men, for I am sure we generally feel very wretched under those circumstances."

" Are you in love, Heinrich?"

He did not reply, but sat by her side silent and looking foolish. With her woman's quick insight she guessed what his thoughts were, and she felt half ashamed of herself for having asked the question.

"Let us talk of something else," he remarked, in a voice which betrayed his emotion.

Lolo seized her cousin's hands, and said, impetuously: " Heinrich, now do not be silly. You must give up serving in a shop; it is not at all suitable for you. You are clever enough, and there are heaps of professions open to you. If you want money I can give you whatever you require, but promise me that you will give up the shop, which I know you hate: continue your studies; enter some profession which will open up to you a career; do not ruin your life through obstinacy in refusing the money I offer you; we are of the same family; should we then not help each other? If I were to ask you to do me a service you would not refuse; why then refuse when I offer to render you one? If you do not like to accept much money, take at least enough to keep you going till you are able to earn a proper livelihood."

" I cannot," he replied. " Do not tempt me, Lolo; I cannot touch your money. My wants are not great; I can earn enough to satisfy them."

" But why will you not take my money ? "

" Do not ask me to explain, Lolo. I cannot tell you ; it is impossible."

" Poor fellow ! " she said, looking at him with pity ; " is there nothing I can do for you ? I am sure you feel unhappy ; you must find the life in the bookseller's shop very dull and depressing."

" I do feel unhappy, Lolo ; but it is no use complaining about it. The best thing to do under the circumstances is to try and forget one's own sorrows by letting one's whole nature be absorbed by interest in some engrossing subject."

" And have you discovered any subject sufficiently interesting to make you forget your own woes, Heinrich ? "

" Yes, I have ; as I have given up all idea of becoming a parson I shall try and do good to my fellow creatures in another way. I have seen the misery there is in this great city ; I will go among the poor whenever I have a leisure moment ; I will try and show them how to ameliorate their condition ; I will hold up to their despairing eyes a possible Utopia ; I will try and rouse them into doing something for themselves ; by preaching in the highways I will do my best to draw the attention of the upper classes to the wants of the poor. Our Government, Lolo, is not perfect, and has much to learn."

" Goodness gracious ! Heinrich, you are not going to become a Democrat or even a Socialist ? You do not mean to say that you aspire to become a deputy ?"

"I do not care, Lolo, to become a deputy; but I see no reason why the voice of the people should not be heard in the streets: men do not worry a government unless they have a real grievance. Call me a Socialist if you like; I do not object to the name. My object is not to carry on war against society; I only wish to try and reform it, to soften down the hard lines which divide classes. I would like to draw down the upper classes a little, so that the distance between them and the lower ones might be lessened by a bit. I do not wish any harm to the Emperor; he is a good man, but he is elevated too high above us to hear the cry of the poor, except as a faint and distant echo."

"Poor fellow," said Lolo, with a voice which expressed real pity for him; "you are quite gone mad, Heinrich, quite mad. You work too hard; you should give up reading all those silly books on politics. I am sure no good ever came of them. Even as a boy I remember you used to have wild theories about government; and did not my father often warn you that if you continued like that you would never come to any good? I am sure you feel tired, and you look overworked." She put her hand to his forehead, which was burning.

"It is quite true, Lolo, I often do feel tired out, and it would be a great pleasure and relief to me if you would allow me to come sometimes when you are not occupied and listen to your singing. I would not trouble you very often."

"Certainly," she replied at once; "come whenever you like. Would you like me to sing to you now?"

"I was afraid to ask you," he said.

She went to the piano in the adjoining room and began singing some of the Italian songs which she remembered he was fondest of in the old days. He remained seated on the couch, and while listening to the well-known tunes he fell into a reverie, recalling to mind the poorly furnished apartment of Lolo's father—the many evenings he had spent there as a boy, when he had been able to escape from his father's house—the discussions on politics and art which used to take place over the beer and scanty supper—the Bohemian society he used to meet there —his boyish dream that he would one day be married to Lolo, which had been so far from realised that he found her now in a sumptuous apartment furnished in Louis XV. style and surrounded with costly bric-à-brac.

The opening of a door woke him from his reverie; it was the nurse who had entered carrying the child. The sight of the infant brought him back to the reality of things; it was like a shock which dispelled all illusions;—Lolo was no longer the girl he had known, but a mother and another man's property. He gave a sigh, and rising from the couch went up to the nurse. He took the babe into his arms, and after looking at her for some time, kissed her and placed her back gently into the nurse's arms. What would he not have given to have had that child his own! Then he took up his hat, and went out on tiptoe without saying a word and without disturbing Lolo, who was still playing the piano and singing in the adjoining room. He was afraid to speak, for he felt that he would have cried.

CHAPTER XIX.

LATE on a winter's night Heinrich Lazarus returned to his garret on the fifth floor of a house in one of the poor quarters of Berlin. He was accompanied by his two inseparable companions, the paint r Ludwig Krause and the student Bernard Adler. He was evidently depressed and in bad humour, and the three companions mounted the long and creaking staircase in silence. When he had reached the topmost floor Heinrich pulled out a key, and unlocking the door entered his room. It was a poorly furnished apartment ; a low bed in one corner, a rough wooden table in the middle of the room, and a few broken chairs about. The whiteness of the snow on the adjoining roofs reflected a faint light sufficient to enable one to distinguish a petroleum lamp upon the table, which, after fumbling in his pocket for some matches, Heinrich succeeded in lighting. It was very cold in that garret under the snow-covered roof without a fire, and with the east wind blowing through the chinks of the ill-fitting window. Heinrich Lazarus threw himself at full length on his bed, while his companions, with their cloaks tightly drawn round them, seated themselves best they could on the broken chairs and began puffing great clouds of smoke from the pipes which they had brought with them.

They had just returned from a socialistic meeting
which had been held in a large room in one of the
low quarters of Berlin. The meeting had begun
orderly enough : at first the speeches, though sufficiently
denunciatory of the powers that be, had still been
couched in fairly decent language, and the police
agent who has to be present at every meeting had
allowed them to pass without any comments beyond
a contemptuous smile ; but after a large amount of
beer and tobacco had been consumed, the heads of
some of the ardent politicians present began to grow
heated, the language used became more and more
violent and anarchic, and finally the representative of
the police thought it his duty to declare the meeting
closed. No sooner had he cut short the oratory of
the would-be politicians than a tumult arose, tables
were upset, and many a beer pot came to an untimely
end through a too violent contact with the floor. A
posse of police, always within call whenever a meeting
is to take place, entered the building, and after a
sharp tussle the beery multitude of orators, politicians,
and idlers was ignominiously ejected into the street,
and the censor of public meetings having locked the
door of the establishment went home well satisfied
with his work, but blaming himself a little for having
listened so long to what he considered the mere
vapouring of fools.

"I will never do it again. I shall never attend any
more of these odious meetings. The people one meets
there are revolting. It is heartrending," sighed
Heinrich from under the blankets which he had
drawn over himself on the bed.

"Heinrich, you are too given to idealism," replied Bernard Adler. "You expect to find educated and refined people at a low meeting like the one we attended to-night. It is very foolish on your part. You must take the working classes as they are, and not look for philosophers amongst them."

"I do not ask for philosophers," exclaimed Heinrich, jumping up from the bed, and beginning to pace his room as he spoke with vehemence. "I do not even ask for educated men; but what disgusts me is to find nothing but egotism, brutality, coarseness, and narrow-mindedness in those blatant orators at popular meetings and would-be leaders of the working classes. Do you know why the social movement in Germany is a failure, and why the aspirations and wants of the common people can be treated with such contempt by Bismarck? I will tell you. It is due to the fact that, with the exception of one or two, our leaders are not sincere, the working classes do not even trust them; they are men with ridiculous ambitions; they are violent but to attract attention; they denounce everything and everybody without hesitation and without thinking; they deliberately delude their uneducated hearers; they promise them the impossible; they want to be talked about; they want to be something, they who ought to be nothing; they pine to be elected to the Reichstag; they dream of becoming ministers; but as for a programme, as for any practical plan for bringing about desirable reforms, as for any scheme for raising the condition of the lower classes, they have none, nor do they care to have one, for they are not sincere. And because we have unfortunately but venal leaders, our poor country has to bow beneath the tyranny of one man, and only occasionally gives forth a spasmodic murmur. It is heartrending to think that the destinies of forty millions of inhabitants should be in the hands of Bismarck. What liberty have we left? We cannot even express our opinions in public without his police agents being there to bully us and to suppress us. What is the Reichstag but a farce? The members may talk a great deal, but when it comes to voting they do as the Chancellor tells them. He has his way in everything. Like the Sultan of Turkey, he sits afar from men, and from his solitude he issues his commands, and they are obeyed. Why, indeed, should a god show himself to the vulgar crowd? When Zeus was angry he thundered, and all men understood and did their best to appease him. What has this man done that he should have this power? It is true that he has united Germany, that he has enlarged our frontiers, that he has re-created the empire; but at what a cost! Individual liberty is gone; a man becomes but a unit of no consequence by itself; everything is sacrificed to the army; the three best years of our lives must be spent shouldering a musket till our hearts grow wearied and heavy, and we resign ourselves to becoming mere machines. Why do we require so large an army, the cost of maintaining which crushes out the spirit of the nation? Is it in order to maintain our own? No! It is that we may frighten France, that we may threaten Russia, that we may act as the bullies of Europe. What the country wants is peace and quiet, relief from crushing taxation, freedom for the individual, restriction of the powers of the police, and an army only sufficiently large to keep out the invader. Bismarck's policy is just the reverse: he has made himself the master here; he has crushed every one who opposed him; now he wants to be the master of the world; he wishes to be able to dictate to foreign countries what their policy shall be. He has made the empire, therefore the Emperor's hands must be strengthened, for is he not his toy? To that end every other consideration must be sacrificed. It is as if Germany had been made for the Emperor, and the Emperor for Bismarck, and not the Emperor and Bismarck for Germany."

The vehemence with which Heinrich Lazarus had declaimed against the Government had brought beads of perspiration upon his brow, and, as he sat down again on the bed, he drew out his pocket-handkerchief and wiped his forehead.

"My dear Heinrich," remarked the painter, "you would do much better to give up politics, they will lead you to no good. Do not go and run your head against a wall. You yourself say that these public meetings are revolting; I quite agree with you, and I certainly shall not attend any more. I shall eschew politics for the future, and I should advise you to do the same. I intend to entirely give myself up to painting, which is a much more interesting subject."

"It is impossible," replied Heinrich; "every man does the best he can. You are born an artist, thank God for it, you have your occupation; I also require one, and it must be one which will absorb all my energies and all my thoughts. I cannot give up politics."

"Heinrich, you are quite right," broke in Bernard Adler; "for young men like ourselves, who do not possess a penny in the world, the only career which can lead us to anything is that of politics. Who knows but that, with perseverance and determination, we may not some day be elected to the Reichstag? Once we are there there is no reason why we should not become ministers, for remember the Bismarck *régime* cannot last for ever; once he is dead, the Reichstag will gain in importance, and the Liberal party will come to power."

"Bernard!" exclaimed Heinrich, with disgust, "you are so very materialistic; you think of nothing but the advantages offered by a political career; you do not care about the nobility of the cause we are espousing, or of the crying wants of the working classes; you engage in the fray for personal reasons, not for the cause itself."

"There is no doubt some truth in what you say, Heinrich," replied Bernard; "but you should remember that if a man did not look after his own interests nobody else would, and that the wise man is the one who, while serving a noble cause, yet takes care to look after himself. Fine sentiments are all very well in their proper place, but fine sentiments do not stir the world; to achieve great things you require the development of that energy which can only be roused by the prospect of personal gain. If you remain gaping at the sky with your mouth open you may be sure that roasted thrushes will not drop into it, however beautiful your thoughts may be, and your stomach will remain hungry and dissatisfied. I think you would be of more use to our fellow creatures if you laboured a little to earn wholesome food to satisfy the natural cravings of your stomach, although thereby the beauty of your thoughts might be somewhat impaired."

" You are just as bad and insincere as any of those violent and bloodthirsty orators who delude the poor, ignorant working classes," said Heinrich, excitedly. " You see no harm in rousing the evil passions of the lower classes, in stirring up the latent envy which is in them of all that is better and more noble than themselves ; you would advocate political murder, if you thought your audience approved of it ; you would promise anything so long as you obtained votes thereby. I believe you would sacrifice everything, your scruples, your principles, your sense of honour, so long as you were elected to the Reichstag. Your ambition is to be there, and, in order to get there, you are capable of perpetrating every turpitude and every deception."

" You are very hard on me, my dear Heinrich," replied Bernard Adler, very quietly. " I grant you that I am not a saint ; but that is no reason for making out that I am a devil. I have got legitimate ambitions. I was unfortunately born almost in the gutter, and I have to fight my own way in the world ; a generous government supplied me with an education equal to that received by the well-to-do classes, but has not extended its generosity far enough so as to supply me with the means of leading a life in con-

formity with my education. I have been crammed
with the classics, my imagination has been fired with
the glories of the world; I have been taught to be
fastidious in my tastes, and now I am told to be
satisfied with bread, sauerkraut, and beer. I am
not content. If you start a large conflagration you do
not expect to extinguish it with a mopping sponge;
my ambition has been fired, and I do not intend to let
it be extinguished with small beer."

"You are a cynic," moaned Heinrich, in a pitiful
voice; "you care for no one but yourself; you have no
sympathy for the poor."

"If it is cynical to see things as they are, and
not allow oneself to be deluded by one's fancies, then
I have no objection to the term," retorted Bernard.
"As for saying that I have no sympathy with the
poor, it is nonsense, for am I not of their number? do
I not know the misery of poverty, the depression it
gives rise to? have I not often felt my nostrils irritated by the smell of a succulent dish as I pass some
eating-shop at a time when my stomach is empty,
and I have not got a penny in my pocket? Do I not
know the envy and evil passions which are roused in
one when one sees one's neighbour in a good coat,
while one's own is torn and one's boots are down at
heel? I sympathise with the poor more than you
think, though I do not cry over them; I would better
their lot just as I would better my own. I am perfectly ready to serve their cause, because in doing so
I serve my purpose, and hope to better my condition."

"Just so," replied Heinrich; "if it were not for the
hope of reward you would do nothing. As I said before,

your object is to get into the Reichstag; and to do so you are ready to promise anything to the electors to get their votes. I am sure you would not hesitate for a moment to consider whether you could perform what you had promised, and you call yourself a friend of the working classes!"

"No doubt in a contest I would promise many things which I knew I could not perform once I was elected," replied Bernard. "I do not pretend that it is very honourable to do so, but then, I did not make the world, nor am I responsible for the foolishness of mankind. Perhaps you would prefer to tell them the naked truth in a brutal way; you would inform them that they must hope for little; that reforms come slowly; that evils of long standing are not remedied in a day. Do you think that they would thank you for your candour? No; they would go back to their beds disheartened and miserable. I would act on a different principle: my first object is to get their votes; my second is to serve their cause, and I will do so to the best of my ability once I am in the Reichstag. How do I proceed? I know their wishes. They want higher wages with less labour, I promise them that they shall have them; they pine for luxuries, I assure them that they shall be lavished upon them; they desire to be possessed of their neighbour's property, I tell them that it is a reasonable wish; they feel envious of the rich, I point out to them that if they elect me I will see that they ride in gilt coaches, and that the rich shall be their slaves. Men are like children; they pine after illusions, and are only happy when they are gulled. You prefer to tell

them the truth, and to accentuate it, so that when
they return home they may the more vividly realise
the pleasures which await them—a jaded wife, brawl-
ing children, and an empty plate for supper. I would
rather fire their imaginations, stuff them with impossible hopes, let them return home to glorious
dreams, so that they might wake on the morrow
more fitted for their work, and better men."

"In the long run deception never answers," replied
Heinrich, "for it is wrong in itself. I begin to believe,
Bernard, that you are devoid of all moral sense. Are
there any limits to the deceptions you would practise?
I suppose not, for once one is embarked upon that
course one is carried along by a current which is too
strong to be resisted. You will begin by lightly promising one thing to your deluded hearers ; but when
the time comes for the fulfilment of the promise, and
you find it impossible to do so, you will cap it by some
further promise still more monstrous and impossible.
One deception leads to another. As you feed the
hopes of your hearers so their appetites will grow ;
then, when you are driven into a corner, as a last resource, you will counsel violence—political murder and
crimes of all sorts—as the simplest way to the realisa-
tion of all you have promised them, and as the best
step towards the regeneration of the working classes."

"My dear Heinrich," replied Bernard Adler, "I am
not a prophet ; I cannot foresee the future ; I am
essentially practical, and only look to the present. To
the making of what promises, or to the giving of what
advice I may be driven to ultimately, interests me for
the moment very little. That some day I may have

to counsel violence is a possibility which I do not deny, and it does not frighten me ; that moment has not yet come, and should it ever arise, it will be because I have then come to the conclusion that violence is the best policy to follow."

" What you say is abominable!" cried Heinrich, with an expression of pain on his face. " A crime is always a crime, and leads to no good."

Bernard Adler replied with a somewhat irritating calmness of manner. " My dear Heinrich, you are rather sweeping in your denunciations. It seems to me that you forget that it was Hödel's pistol and the pellets of Nöbeling's gun which first brought the wrongs of the working classes in Germany vividly before the eyes of the world, and that it is only since the two attempts on the Emperor's life that Bismarck has turned his attention to the sufferings of the working classes, and begun to legislate for their relief. So you see that sometimes what you call a crime may lead to some good."

" Never ! " exclaimed Heinrich Lazarus, emphatically. " I have studied theology, and I know how fallacious is that plausible doctrine of the Jesuits that the end justifies the means."

" I cannot see how any sensible man can object to the doctrine," remarked Bernard Adler ; " the only difference of opinion which can exist is as to the nobility of the end. Granted that the end for which you are working is noble, then the means which are necessary for attaining that end are sanctified by its nobility ; for surely an action is not good or evil in itself, but only relatively to the end for which it was perpetrated. The men who are nervously and timidly scrupulous never come to anything in this world."

"I deny that absolutely!" screamed Heinrich, as he jumped up from his bed and began gesticulating with much vehemence; "there is no truth in all you say. There are men who believe in truth and honesty and nobility of conduct; men who are unselfish and ready to sacrifice everything for the good of their fellow creatures without hoping for any reward. You may call them fools and enthusiasts; you say that they achieve nothing in this world;— I deny it. Their very self-abnegation makes them conquer the world. Look at the apostles and the early Christian martyrs; look at the founders of religious faiths; look at the missionaries who have braved dangers and death in the discharge of what they consider to be their duty; if you want a modern example, look at Gordon." (It was the winter when the British troops were approaching Khartoum, and General Gordon's name was in everybody's mouth.)

"I am not well read in Church history," replied Bernard Adler; "but it seems to me that even the apostles did not give themselves all the trouble they are reputed to have done without some hope of reward. It was not so much the fear of hell as the hope of heaven which spurred them on to all their exertions, and I strongly suspect that they expected the coming of the kingdom of heaven in the immediate future, and that is why they were in such a hurry to earn their reward; nor have we any reasons to suppose that they believed that material joys and worldly advantages would be banished from its realm."

"You are getting blasphemous," retorted Heinrich, who had been trained for the Church, and who had not yet lost all his beliefs.

"Well, my dear Heinrich," continued Bernard, "I shall leave the apostles alone, and come to your modern example of a self-denying man, who works only for the good of his fellow creatures, and never thinks of himself. I do not pretend to know more about Gordon than what I have read about him in the papers, but that is sufficient for my purpose. Let us consider his career, and what he has done. As a young man, the British Government lend him to the Chinese authorities to put down a rebellion. I will suppose that in accepting this duty he acted on the best of motives, and that he had really considered the rights and wrongs of the case, and that he had come to the conclusion that the rebels were so entirely in the wrong that they ought for the good of humanity to be extirpated. I do not blame him so very much if he erred in judgment, for men are not infallible; but it seems to me hardly credible that several millions of inhabitants would take up arms against a Government out of sheer wantonness, and not because they had suffered intolerable oppression. One may well ask, however, why your typical Christian hero should go out of his way to interfere in other people's affairs; surely such conduct is blameworthy, and if frequently indulged in, is it not likely to lead to much friction and irritation in this world? You may call this a side issue; well, let

us examine what Gordon actually did. He crushed
the rebellion ; he destroyed cities ; he killed thousands
of people. Are these Christian acts in themselves ?
Do they not rather resemble what we might expect
from a professional brigand or from the condottieri
in the Middle Ages, men who were ever ready without
a scruple to sell their services to any government ?
You will no doubt answer that these laboured for
money, whereas Gordon gave his services to the
Chinese Government with no expectation of pecuniary
reward, that he entered upon this work because he
considered it to be his duty to do so, and that to put
an end to a long-standing rebellion was a noble thing.
I reply that the intention can in no wise affect the
deed, and that to do harm that good may come of
it is but the principle you condemned a moment ago
that the end justifies the means. Admire Gordon
for crushing the Taeping rebellion and you are bound
to make of Torquemada a saint."

"Then you admire nothing in Gordon ? " asked
Heinrich, with a look of supreme disgust on his
face.

"You are mistaken," replied Bernard ; " I admire
a great deal in the man ; I admire his valour, his
perseverance, his dogged determination to succeed,
his resource in difficulties, his great military talent.
I admire these qualities in him, just as I admire them
in Napoleon ; but I do not think that they are rendered
the more attractive because your Christian hero
carries a Bible under his arm, speaks contemptuously
of the earth, and only looks forward to obtaining his
reward in heaven."

" Reward ! reward ! always harping on reward ! "
ejaculated Heinrich, who was getting irritated at
the turn the conversation had taken.

" Prospect of reward in some form or other is the
motive power in man. Would you expect a steam
engine to work if you put no fuel into it ? " asked
Bernard Adler.

" I suppose you will tell me next that Gordon went
to Khartoum only to obtain a reward ? " remarked
Heinrich, with a sneer.

" The reward of the enthusiast," replied Bernard,
" lies in the calm indifference, similar to that of the
opium drinker's, to all worldly things, coupled with
that pleasurable satisfaction which comes of a firm
belief in the justice of all one does, and then crown of
all reward the ecstatic gaze towards a divine future.
Look at the Arab conquerors in the early days of
Mahomedanism ; did they not court death so as to
pass from a world of sorrows to reap their reward
in a carnal heaven ? I would do the same if I believed
in the reality of the thing. To Gordon heaven
appears in a more spiritual light than to the Arabs ;
but still it is a living reality to him, and so he is
ready to shuffle off this mortal coil as soon as possible
to get there. Do not tell me that your religious
enthusiast does not work without feeling any pleasure
or without having his eyes turned towards a prospect
of reward. The only difference which I can see
between what we will call a typical Christian hero
and an ordinary man is, that the ordinary man looks
for his reward in this world, whereas your hero defers
it until after death. It seems to me to be nothing

LIBRARY
UNIVERSITY OF ILLINOIS

more than a technical difference such as that between a bill at short date and a bill at long date."

"This is all sophistry!" shouted Heinrich; "you will not make the world believe that enthusiasm is ridiculous, and that Gordon's self-sacrificing and noble mission to Khartoum is blameworthy."

"No doubt," replied Bernard, "enthusiasm is a great motive power in the world, but if it is not directed by sane men it will probably do a great deal more harm than good. The papers tell us that Gordon went to Khartoum for two purposes: the first to bring about the withdrawal of the Egyptian garrison; the second to try and save the Soudan if it is possible from anarchy. Like an enthusiast, he rushes off wildly to carry out his mission; he believes that he alone can save the situation, that his prestige will enable him to restore order in the Soudan. Of course the British Government is delighted to make use of him; not that the practical persons in power really believe that he can do much, but in order to quiet public clamour for the moment, and they trust to luck to get him out of his difficulties. So your enthusiast is employed, and what comes of it? He gets to Khartoum; he declines to carry out his instructions of withdrawing the Egyptian troops and to come away with them; he calls it a shame and a disgrace to abandon the town to the Mahdi, although most of the inhabitants are apparently indifferent about it; but there are a few Christians in the place who might suffer if the Mahdi triumphed, so he will defend the place to the last; he does not seem to care how much suffering is entailed thereby; the supporters of the Mahdi are

looked upon by him as without the bounds of humanity,
and we read in the papers that every day he goes up
the river in his bullet-proof steamers and shoots
Mahdists on the bank with as much calmness as a
sportsman would do partridges. He clamours loudly
for help; fickle public opinion in England is at last
roused; the Government has to give way; an army
is sent out; thousands will be killed, and millions of
money will be spent, and after all who can tell whether
Khartoum will be relieved and the Soudan wrested
from the grasp of the Mahdi? That is what comes when
a government trusts to an enthusiast, and allows him
to have his own way; one blunder leads to another,
and the fatal consequences of letting Gordon go to
Khartoum may be felt for many years to come. I
admire, as I told you already, the bravery with which
he defends the place, though I condemn the reason
for which he holds it; I admire the soldier Gordon,
though I have but little respect for the Christian
hero."

Heinrich, who felt bitterly the attack made by his
friend on his ideal hero Gordon, replied: "You may
call it logic to argue as you have done, and to traduce
every action of a hero like Gordon, but to me it seems
to show nothing but cold-blooded cynicism. Perhaps
you may succeed in the world by guiding your conduct
on the principles you have expounded, but I prefer
to fail in holding ever before my eyes a perhaps
unrealisable ideal. I mean to dedicate my life to
the service of the working classes; I will labour in
their cause; I will do my best to point out the way
towards progress and advancement by legal and moral

means; I will try and infuse into them faith in themselves: I will raise their spirits and rouse their energies, and I hope that efforts like these may some day make the world a more noble place to dwell in than at present: then social frictions shall have been toned down; the bitter hatred between class and class shall have disappeared; to do a good action will no longer arouse sneers and ridicule, and perhaps then the State will have stepped in to prevent the cruel and degrading competition between trades by which the artisan is reduced to slavery. I believe that these things can be done, and I will work towards their attainment." He would have continued speaking had not the petroleum lamp, after flickering for a few moments, gone out and left them in the dark. A wintry moon in its last quarter shed a faint light into the room. The painter Ludwig Krause had been asleep in his chair for some time.

"It is late," remarked Bernard Adler, "and time to break up; we shall continue the discussion another day. Ludwig!" he exclaimed, giving the sleeping painter a friendly slap on the back, "wake up, and come along with me; it is time to go to bed."

Ludwig Krause stretched himself and yawned. "I suppose you have been discussing politics whilst I have been asleep; it is the last thing I can remember before I began to doze. What eager politicians you both are, to be sure! I have been better employed; I have been dreaming of my model, only she was so much prettier in the dream than in reality."

Heinrich struck a match against the wall, and showed his friends the way downstairs; he opened the house door to let them out, and after saying good-night he returned to his solitary and dark room. Throwing himself upon the bed he recalled to mind with disgust the rowdy meeting he had attended ; then he felt overcome with a sickening feeling of despair because not even his own friends seemed to sympathise with his aspirations, and he thought how differently things might have been if he had acceded to his father's wish that he should enter the Church and had been able to marry Lolo. He burst into tears as he thought of the hopelessness of his prospects, till at last, tired out with the day's work, he fell asleep.

CHAPTER XX.

HEINRICH passed a restless night. As soon as it was daylight he rose, with his head still full of the political conversation of the previous evening. He made a hasty toilet, and finding the solitude of his chamber unbearable he resolved to go out. When he reached the bottom of the staircase he found the cobler August Busse already at work in his little shop on the ground floor.

"Good-morning, Herr Lazarus," shouted the cobler in his gruff voice, continuing all the while to repair a boot which he held in his hand. "You are up early to-day, though you came home late last night. You seem to have carried on a pretty lively discussion with your friends, for though you live on the top floor I heard your voices down here. Late hours are bad things for young men."

"We were discussing politics, August; it is better to give up a little sleep to discuss great subjects than to oversleep oneself and so grow stupefied."

"He who sleeps well works well," replied the cobler. "You young fellows are too much engaged in discussing politics; you argue, gesticulate, and shout a great deal, as if the world were likely to be influenced by your views. You would be more profitably engaged in doing honest work and talking less."

" It is not by keeping your nose in the gutter that you can elevate your soul. It is not by indifference to great subjects that mankind has made progress," replied Heinrich, with a look of contempt at the cobler. " It would do you no harm, August, if you would sometimes turn your attention from the cobbling of old boots to the contemplation of great social questions."

" And what good would it do me?" grunted August Busse, without so much as lifting his face from his work. " It seems to me that there are quite enough men already who indulge in nothing but talk, and who contemplate your great social questions, and what comes of it all ? "

" It is only by ventilating grievances that you get any attention paid to them," remarked Heinrich. " No government will trouble itself to find a remedy for evils unless those evils are thrust upon its notice by agitation and public discussion. By resignation and silence one only earns contempt."

" I have got no grievance against the Government," retorted the cobbler ; "taxes no doubt are heavy, but still things go well enough with me, and I do not complain ; and supposing I did indulge in grumbling, what good would it do me ? "

" No grievances against the Government ? " asked Heinrich, with a look of pity at the cobbler. " If you have no grievances, it only shows that you are too dull to notice them. Every man must have grievances, and even if you are too indolent to care about your own, as a good citizen you might take some interest in those of your neighbours."

"Young man," growled the burly cobbler, "are you going to teach me what are the duties of a good citizen? Your education is no doubt better than mine, but I was present at Sadowa; I went through the whole of the French campaign; I have done something for the fatherland. You may have your head full of beautiful theories, which I am too ignorant to understand, but I have something which is better than theories, and that is experience; and I can tell you, Herr Lazarus, that this Government of ours is a very good Government, and we ought to be very thankful that we live under it, and so long live Bismarck and the Emperor." August Busse raised his morning pot of beer, which was by his side, and took a long pull at its contents.

"I suppose you never read the newspapers?" remarked Heinrich, contemptuously.

"I very rarely do; it costs too much money to buy them, and I hear all the news at the 'Bierhalle.'"

"Then if you really hear the news, August, you must be aware that Bismarck is ruining the prosperity of Germany by his abominable protective system; that he has fostered industries artificially which cannot last and are certain to come to grief; that the sugar production of the country is being ruined by the bounty system; that agriculture is languishing and trade generally dull." Heinrich was at that time an enthusiastic free trader, for he had lately been studying Mill's "Political Economy" and the works of other English economists.

"Herr Lazarus," answered the cobler, looking up at his interlocutor, "do you expect me to believe that the Emperor does not know his business, and that if he puts his trust in Prince Bismarck it is without good reason, and without having first carefully considered the interests of the nation? Young man, you have still much to learn which is not to be found in books. If trade is in as bad a way as you make out, who tells you that the fault lies with the Chancellor, and that it is not due to natural causes? Anyhow, the subject does not interest me much, for under whatever government I may have to live men will continue to wear out their boots and to want them repaired. I am doing fairly well, and do not find my trade depressed." August Busse took another pull at his pot of beer, then with much energy and apparent satisfaction to himself he brought down the mallet he was holding in his hand and drove a tack into the sole of the boot he was repairing.

" Stupid, uninteresting lout," muttered Heinrich, as he walked away thinking to himself how much rousing the working classes needed before they would pay an intelligent attention to public affairs and look beyond the petty interests of their own trade. It was too early for him to go to his bookseller's shop in the Unter den Linden, so he strolled about the streets revolving problems in his mind how to elevate the lower classes, and feeling all the while very much depressed. He passed a coffee shop, and having taken nothing that morning he went in. It was a dingy room, in which the smell of stale tobacco smoke prevailed ; a few workmen were sitting at tables sipping hot coffee. Heinrich ordered some, and seeing a man looking more intelligent than the others he went and sat by his side.

"Cold morning," said the stranger to Heinrich.

"Yes, it is indeed," he replied ; " these coffee shops are excellent things for the working classes ; they enable them to get something warm at a small cost."

"Good enough in cold weather," answered the stranger : " but I must say that I do not often patronise temperance establishments. I believe in strong drinks and plenty of them. Your regular coffee drinker is no use at all ; he is always effete ; there's no stuff in him. I always drink a great deal, it keeps my spirits up."

"You must be engaged in a flourishing business, if you can throw away so much money in drinking," said Heinrich to his neighbour.

"Pretty lucrative business mine," answered the stranger, with a cynical laugh.

"I congratulate you," replied Heinrich ; " I thought Bismarck with his abominable protective system had ruined every trade in Germany ; I am glad to find that there are still a few which have survived in spite of his policy."

"If Bismarck has really ruined German trade God thank him for it," retorted the stranger ; " for when trade is generally dull money comes into my pocket."

"I do not understand you," mumbled Heinrich, who began to feel very much annoyed at his neighbour's tone.

"It is simple enough," continued the stranger ; " when trade is flourishing the daughters of the working men are like the vestal virgins, almost unassailable ; when trade is dull we have no difficulty in engaging them for service abroad. It is a paying business."

" Abominable ! " exclaimed Heinrich, turning round and looking the stranger straight in the face. " Does the police not try to put a stop to your operations ? "

" Oh ! we make the police our friends," replied the stranger, with a sneer.

" It is intolerable," said Heinrich, rising from his seat ; " it is intolerable to have to live under a police *régime*, but it is ten times worse when the police waste their time in bullying inoffensive persons, and then close their eyes to crimes such as yours." The stranger blew a puff of smoke into Heinrich's face which made him cough and stopped his harangue. Heinrich paid for his coffee, and then left the shop more depressed than when he entered it, muttering to himself that it was disheartening to find that among the lower classes the intelligent-looking ones were vicious, while the honest ones were stupid. He walked to the shop where he was employed, and tried to drive away his thoughts by reading in the intervals when he was not engaged in handing over the counter to some pretty countess the last new vicious novel from Paris.

In the evening the three friends met again in the small studio where Ludwig Krause slept and painted. They were seated round a table eating a meagre repast, which they washed down with copious draughts of frothy beer.

" My dear fellow," said the painter, making the vault of the studio ring with his loud voice, " I am in luck to day, for I have sold a picture for a very reasonable sum." They made their mugs clink, and then they drank to Ludwig Krause's health and wished him further successes.

" Is it not far more sensible to eat and drink and
be merry as we are now, than to attend socialistic
meetings ? there one runs every chance of getting one's
head broken, and of being eventually chucked out by
the police."

" You forget, Ludwig," remarked Bernard Adler,
" that politics are to be my profession as well as Heinrich's, and that although to attend socialistic meetings
may not be very agreeable, yet it is a necessity for us
to do so unless we wish to remain in obscurity."

" If I were you," replied Ludwig, " I would give
up that ridiculous desire to get into the Reichstag.
No respectable man wants to be elected to it ; it is
the largest collection of educated nonentities to be
found in the world. The members talk a great deal,
but no one pays much attention to them, and they have
no power. Politics are very well as a pastime for
men of fortune, but they are of no use as a profession
to poor devils like ourselves."

" I do not at all agree with you," said Bernard Adler,
with some warmth ; " there is no profession which
gives you so many opportunities of advancement as
politics ; in all other professions you can advance to
the top of the tree only slowly and by steady work ;
in politics youth is no bar to success ; all that is
required, if you want to succeed, is a certain amount
of cleverness, or rather smartness, great determination,
and the instinct never to lose a chance of advertising
and drawing attention to oneself. Moreover, politics
taken up seriously give you the satisfaction of feeling
yourself engaged in the fray of public life ; your name
appears in the newspapers ; you hear men talking

about you ; is that not more exhilarating than to have
to sit behind a desk all day long copying other people's
remarks or adding up accounts ? ”

“ To lead such a life may be very amusing,” remarked the painter, “ but it does not bring in much
money, and the body requires to be clothed and fed.”

“ Money is not everything,” replied Bernard ; “ but
you are mistaken if you think that I propose entering
the political arena merely to acquire fame, and without
a hope of obtaining some more material recompense
for my pains. The essential point is to make a splash,
then one of two things will probably occur : the
Government of the day will begin to bully you, ill-treat
you, possibly imprison you, then immediately the
purses of your adherents will be opened, and a nice
and comfortable subscription presented to you because
you have not feared to suffer for the cause ; this is
very comfortable, for by putting up for a small time
with the inconveniences of a prison life you emerge
with reputation increased, coupled with a considerable
pecuniary reward. The other case which may arise is
to my mind still more satisfactory ; having made
yourself exceedingly disagreeable to the Government,
you will find, probably, that attempts will be made to
bribe you to keep quiet ; if you are not unreasonable, the
matter will be arranged and you will be given a good
berth ; you may in this way secure for yourself a situation
in a Government department without having had the
trouble of going through the drudgery of beginning at
the foot of the ladder of the bureaucratic hierarchy.”

“ If a man acted like that I would call him a blackguard,” exclaimed Heinrich.

"It is very easy and very foolish to call people
names," answered Bernard Adler; "but it seems to
me that a man who enters Government service has so
many more opportunities of doing good than a person
who out of pigheadedness prefers to remain outside
and to indulge in clamour and opposition, that to
refuse an opening would be exceedingly foolish on his
part. To indulge in clamour and opposition with **an**
ulterior object in view, I can understand; but clamour
for its own sake seems to me ridiculous, and I must
say I have **great contempt** for the man who poses
as a martyr when there is no necessity for him **to
do so.**"

"It is **lucky that the great** leaders **of** the democratic
party are not **of your opinion**," said Heinrich. "It is
not by deception **that great** causes are furthered; it is
only by being **honest and** straightforward, as well as
reasonable **in** their demands, that the leaders of the
working classes will command attention and respect
for the cause they advocate. Every leader who turns
dishonest damages the cause of **the** working classes
immeasurably."

"Intellectually **the** greatest leader the German
democracy **ever** had **was** undoubtedly Lasalle,"
remarked Bernard, " and you always told me, Heinrich,
that you admired **him** immensely; well, I am convinced that if he had not been unfortunately killed
in a duel he **would now** be working hand in hand with
Bismarck **in** consolidating the power of the Emperor;
he would have developed **into** one of the pillars of
the State, and become one of the great supporters of
the one-man rule."

" Bernard, do not calumniate the dead ! " shouted Heinrich across the table.

" I do not calumniate any one," retorted Bernard ; " I have studied Lasalle's works, and the conclusion I have come to is that he would have supported the strong hand in government, for it is only where a strong personality has absolute power that great reforms can be carried out. I admire Lasalle for many reasons, and for none more than because he loved women. Whatever a man may do, I will always judge him leniently if he gets killed in a duel defending the lost honour of his mistress."

" Quite right, Bernard ; there is nothing in the world so interesting as women ! " exclaimed the painter, casting a loving look at the study of a nude female which hung on the wall : it was not the portrait of some kitchen wench about to take a bath, but Ludwig Krause's idea of what a nymph might have been in classic days.

For a time the conversation flagged, and the three friends seemed to be more busy in satisfying their hunger than in discussing great subjects. Suddenly Heinrich jumped up in a state of considerable excitement, and exclaimed as he began pacing the room : " I have had an idea for some time, but I have been afraid to tell it you, for Bernard is so cynical that he is certain to turn it into ridicule."

" Impossible, my dear fellow," answered Bernard, laughing.

" Let us hear your idea," said the painter, " and if it is a good one, I will send and pay for another jug of beer."

"I have been thinking for some time upon the difficulties which lie in the path of reform in Germany," began Heinrich. "In contemplating the political situation here with that in foreign countries, what strikes one as so strange is, that we should still find in Germany remnants of the feudal system permeating the people, such as the sharp line which still divides the nobility from the remainder of the nation, and the fact that we look upon a barbarous military life as the one to which all that is noblest in the land should aspire. The antiquated ideas which govern our social life must be changed to the very core : we must liberate the man just as was done in France by the Revolution : we must make him understand his own dignity, make him feel that as man he is the equal of any one, though in worldly goods all may not be endowed alike ; we must show him that it only depends upon himself, by improving his education, by making the most of his natural abilities, to rise to the highest post in the State. We must break down the barriers which exist in Germany, and throw open the road which leads to honours to all who care to exert themselves to march along it."

"Men do not want to be equal," broke in the painter ; "we all think ourselves geniuses and our fellow creatures fools ; we all want to be at the top of the tree, so as to able to look down upon the rest of mankind."

"I quite recognise," continued Heinrich, "that though men are equal in the eyes of God, yet in this world they are endowed with different physical and intellectual qualities, and that to keep them artificially equal would mean stagnation ; but what I advocate is that no unnatural impediments be placed in the way of men finding their level, and that the State should not create social distinctions to give a particular individual a lift in the world above his fellows without his having done anything to deserve it. Perhaps you will say that this objection to class distinction is a sentimental one, and that such distinctions do little harm ; it is possibly so, but then one should remember that sentiment plays an important part in the lives of mankind."

"I do not understand what you are driving at," muttered Bernard, with his mouth full of salad made with herrings.

"What I mean," replied Heinrich, " is that inequalities artificially created are one of the chief causes of the irritation which exists between the classes, and that it would be wise to remove as much as possible the causes of this irritation so as to render the discussion of more important reforms less bitter and thereby to facilitate their introduction. It is better to bring about reforms by peaceable means than by revolutions."

"Utopias, my dear Heinrich," said Bernard, " I do not believe for a moment that people who possess wealth, privileges, and other advantages will yield up anything to those who possess nothing unless a pistol is presented at their head. Without riot or threats of violence you will never obtain anything from the aristocracy. In the world of politics every man has to look after himself ; no one cares a hang about his neighbour, unless that neighbour happens to make himself excessively disagreeable."

"I am not of your opinion," replied Heinrich, " and

I think I have told you pretty often how disgusted I felt at the way the leaders of the democratic and socialist parties carry on the campaign against abuses, and the methods they use to draw attention to long-needed reforms. Their advocacy of violence, their general ignorance and want of education, their vulgarity, their noisy declamation, their continual attempts to stir up envy between the classes, and above all their insincerity, damage the cause, cover it with ridicule and contempt, and encourage the well-to-do to turn a deaf ear to the real and terrible sufferings of the working classes and to their just demands for reforms. I would like to alter all that."

"You are very ambitious, my dear Heinrich," remarked Bernard; "and how would you set about to do it?"

"I would use other methods," answered Heinrich, "and perhaps thereby achieve more. What I have been thinking about, and would like to propose, is that we should found a society to which we should attract all the young and enthusiastic students at the universities; that we should agree upon a reasonable and practical programme of reforms; that we should then go into the streets in all the large towns of Germany and preach to the passers-by, not as if we were brigands advocating violence and the pillaging of other men's property, but rather as apostles bearing the olive branch of peace, preaching the gospel of goodwill on earth to all men, drawing the attention of the rich to the sores of Lazarus, and not demanding alms by threats, but by making appeal to the better side of human nature, and doing our best to rouse that pity and enthusiasm to do good, which I believe exist in every man though they are often hidden by selfishness, bad education, and social prejudices. We shall woo attention to our grievances by gentleness, and we shall gain the sympathy even of those who do not agree with us."

For a few minutes Bernard Adler remained staring with astonishment at Heinrich ; then bringing down his fist upon the table he exclaimed with a preliminary oath : "You have more in you, Heinrich, than I ever expected. The idea is splendid ; we shall form a society ; you will supply the enthusiasm ; I will take charge of the more practical department. I will organise the demonstrations, and arrange for their simultaniety in all the large cities of Germany ; I shall also find recruits for the society. We shall have to prepare everything very secretly, and then, when all is ready, on a general holiday, say the Emperor's birthday four months hence, we shall descend into the streets about noon when they will be full of people, and then blaze away at the passers-by with all our eloquence. There is no doubt that we shall be run in by the police, and probably condemned to a few months of prison fare ; but what does that matter ? We shall emerge with reputations made ; the newspapers will be full of us ; there may even be an interpellation in the Reichstag on the subject. What an advertisement it will be ! Just the thing we wanted to lift us out of obscurity. The idea is immense ! Let us set to work at once to put it into execution."

"You are always thinking of personal advantage," said Heinrich ; "you will ruin the scheme."

"I will do nothing of the sort," replied Bernard Adler; "I fully recognise what a powerful lever enthusiasm is for moving people, but you must have a sane practical person to direct the lever; I know heaps of young students who will supply with you the requisite amount of enthusiasm and self-denial. I will get round them, and bring them into the fold. Leave the practical organisation of the scheme to me, and we shall succeed; you will have to employ yourself in supplying a fine-sounding programme; do not forget to clothe your thoughts in magnificent language, for fine language, like good music, intoxicates the hearers. I see you look at me as if you did not approve of what I suggest. Be reasonable, Heinrich, and let yourself be guided by me; do not let your brilliant idea be ruined by a too squeamish examination of the methods we are to employ. We both want to draw the attention of the world to the woes of the working classes so that a remedy may be found for them; we can only do so effectively by being practical, and by not seeking after the impossible. Remember, my dear Heinrich, that to succeed in this world in any big undertaking you must mix one part of what is genuine with at least two parts of what is humbug."

After a few moments of hesitation Heinrich replied in a tone of resignation: "All right, Bernard; do what you think is best." He felt that to succeed in this venture it would be well to let himself be guided, much as he disliked it, by a practical, common-sense person like Bernard, who would not be likely to lose his head or to be carried away by enthusiasm.

"That is very sensible of you, Heinrich," answered

Bernard; "and now, my dear Ludwig, what are you going to do? Will you also join our new society which is to bring salvation to Germany and honour to ourselves?"

"Not such a fool," replied the painter, with his loud, jovial voice; "leave me in peace to paint pictures, and do not ask me to go and get my head broken at public meetings, for that is the fate which is in store for you. You are both of you lunatics, forgive me for saying so. It is no good running counter to a well-established Government; it only brings you into disrepute, which would never do for me, as it would frighten away my clients, and I have few enough of them; and how should I live if nobody bought my pictures? Art is better than politics, and to succeed in art one requires peace and solitude, and not the noise and excitement of political meetings. But, my dear friends, you can talk to me about your secret society as much as you like, as long as you do not ask me to belong to it; so we can continue to be friends, and to see as much of each other as before."

They continued to sit and talk over their beer till a late hour, and when they broke up Heinrich and Bernard walked home in buoyant spirits and full of the grand idea of founding a secret society which would shortly make a great stir in Germany, and perhaps bring about an amelioration of the lot of the working classses.

CHAPTER XXI.

COUNT KLINKENSTEIN was in his rooms and in very bad humour, for his uncle General Count Eckstein was to arrive in Berlin in a few hours' time accompanied by his daughter. It was not that he objected to meeting his cousin Nelly again, for she had left a very pleasant impression upon him, but he felt that it was a bore to have to be continually dancing attendance on his uncle's family, and that their presence in Berlin would interfere a good deal with his freedom, and that he would no longer be able to spend all his evenings with Lolo as he had been accustomed to do of late. So when the time came for him to go to the station like a dutiful nephew to meet his uncle, he enlivened the walk thither by the explosion of a series of oaths which seemed to give considerable relief to his feelings.

With German punctuality the train entered the station, and after the exchange of the warm salutations customary between relatives in Germany, Count Klinkenstein found himself installed in a carriage with his uncle and cousin driving to an hotel, while the servants were left to look after the luggage.

"Of course, Edward, you will come and dine with us to-night?" said the old General to his nephew.

Count Klinkenstein was rather taken aback, as he

had made arrangements for a supper party in Lolo's apartment that night, and he showed by his looks that he did not relish the idea of having to dine with his uncle.

Nelly noticed it, and said : " It is not nice of you to make a face like that, as if you thought it a bore to have to dine with us. You must come ; we see so little of you. I promise you I will make myself as agreeable as I can."

Count Klinkenstein looked up at his cousin, and it seemed to him that she was exceedingly pretty. " Well, Nelly, I will come; but it is only for your sake," he said, " for it is highly inconvenient for me to do so ; and I shall have to leave you very early, as I must attend a supper to-night, which it is impossible for me to miss. I must be there."

" Is it given by particular friends of yours, Edward ? "

" Yes, most particular ones," he replied, colouring a good deal ; but now that he was in for telling fibs, it seemed to him that it did not very much matter how many he told, and the blame was Nelly's for asking such questions.

" Are suppers a common form of entertainment in Berlin ? " inquired Nelly.

" Oh, very common among the officers ; you see the theatres begin so early, generally at seven o'clock, that it is too inconvenient to have to dine before going to them, so we generally put off our dinner to after the play."

" I do not like the system," remarked Nelly ; " I have been accustomed to go to bed very early. It must be a great bore to have to stay up very late,

and one must do that if one has suppers, for you know
it is a bad thing to go to bed directly after eating."

"That is quite true, Nelly; but you need not be
alarmed, for in all probability you will not be often
asked to attend such functions."

"Do not ladies go to suppers, then?" inquired Nelly,
quite innocently.

"Yes, they do," replied Count Klinkenstein, blushing,
because of the presence of his uncle, and stammering
a good deal. "Ladies are invited to suppers; but you
see they are not generally very young girls or in good
society."

"Then what sort of persons are they? Is there
anything wrong in going to a supper?"

"No, it is not the supper which is to blame, Nelly,
it is the society which partakes of it. You see at
that hour of night people so frequently become noisy
and forget how to behave, and then the ladies who
go to suppers are generally actresses and ballet-girls,
and you can understand that directly their labours for
the night are over they want to be amused."

"Oh!" exclaimed Nelly, rather astonished; and
then she added: "Edward, are you acquainted with
many actresses?"

"Of course I am, Nelly; a young officer of the
Guards knows all the fashionable actresses; they
are very charming creatures."

"My governess always told me that they were a
very bad lot," answered Nelly, who felt rather annoyed
at her cousin's air of superior knowledge. A look
from the old General gave Count Klinkenstein to
understand that he did not appreciate the turn the

conversation was taking, so there followed a silence of some duration. Presently, as their carriage crossed the Unter den Linden, a very well turned out victoria passed them at a rapid pace.

"Oh! Edward, did you see that smart carriage, and what a pretty woman there was inside it? Do you know who she is?" asked Nelly, with a woman's natural curiosity.

Count Klinkenstein looked round and recognised that the carriage which was driving away fast was Lolo's. He did not quite know what to reply to his cousin's question, so he shrugged his shoulders as if he felt bored at having to answer so silly a question, and merely said: "It is nothing particular, Nelly."

"But it was, Edward. She must be a great lady, for her carriage was so elegant, and she herself was so pretty. Do you know who she is?"

"Only an actress," replied Count Klinkenstein, rather flattered that a woman should recognise the good looks of his mistress, but annoyed, nevertheless, that Nelly should immediately on her arrival in Berlin have run up against Lolo, and should be asking questions about her.

"You must be wrong, Edward," replied Nelly, very deliberately; "she cannot be an actress, for the salaries of actresses are not sufficiently large to allow them to possess a carriage as elegant as the one which passed us."

"You forget, Nelly, that great actresses sometimes make very large fortunes, and that when they have acquired a reputation they are usually surrounded by admirers who are only too pleased to give them anything for which they may express a desire."

"And is she a great actress?" asked Nelly, with a tone of incredulity; "she looked so very young."

"I really did not see who she was," replied Count Klinkenstein. At that moment the carriage drove up to the door of the hotel, and he was very glad to be relieved from having to answer any further questions respecting his mistress.

Count Klinkenstein's sister had resolved to spend the coming winter in Berlin instead of returning to Florence, where her husband was at that moment staying. She had come to this resolution partly because she felt it incumbent upon her to take her cousin Nelly into society, as the old General seemed very much averse to undertaking the duties of a chaperon, and partly because rumours had reached her that her brother was not leading the most reputable life since he had joined the Gardes du Corps; and as she knew his weak character she felt afraid that he might in a moment of foolishness marry some woman of bad repute, and so ruin his career. She herself had no children, and her brother was the last direct representative of the ancient house of Klinkenstein, so it was only natural that she should wish to see him settled down and married respectably. She had never had any taste for military affairs, and she hoped that if her brother got married he might be induced to give up the army and to retire to Klinkenstein, where his presence was badly wanted to look after the property and the people on it. She hoped that her brother would fall in love with Nelly and marry her, and it certainly would have been a desirable match in many ways.

"Edward," said the Countess Gièsle one day to her brother, "are you not yet tired of barrack life and of the society of soldiers and officers ? "

"Not in the least, Gisèle," he replied ; " I am amusing myself immensely. I never imagined when I first came up to Berlin that one could get so much fun out of the place."

"Edward, do you never think of Klinkenstein ? Have you no desire of living there some day ? "

"None whatever," he replied without hesitation ; " it is awfully dull there, absolutely nothing to do in the place, and the village maidens are not even pretty enough to induce a man to make love to them. It was all very well for our barbarous ancestors to go and live in the country in big solemn-looking castles, but it does not suit us nineteenth-century people at all. Nowadays we require to be surrounded by what is bright and lively ; we want continual amusements, and they should be of a frivolous, not a serious nature. My ideal home would be a bright little villa, luxuriously furnished with dainty frail chairs and tables, not solid furniture in the old German style, which was meant to last for generations ; the curtains and hangings should be of silk, of light and delicate tints ; the bed would be a poem in inlaid rosewood, with a pale blue ceiling ; round the house there ought to be a garden, not necessarily large, but having a few big shady trees, and there ought to be arbours in retired nooks, and a splashing fountain or two, for it is very refreshing to listen to the sound of falling water on a hot day. Moreover, the villa ought to be near a town, not buried in the country, for I like to see people about me, and to hear the movement of humanity, for I hate solitude; and then, most important point of all, Gisèle, I would require a very pretty woman in my house as a companion."

"Do you mean as a wife, Edward?"

"Of course I do; in what other sense could you take it, Gisèle? Do you suppose I am quite an abandoned person? Besides, I could not live in a house with a girl I did not love, and if I loved her I suppose I would marry her."

"Edward, why do you not marry, and then build your ideal house? It would be a more pleasant occupation, I am sure, than to be continually drilling troops."

"I have told you already that I am very fond of a military life and of the beautiful city of Berlin; besides, Gisèle, I do not see why I should be in such a hurry to build my ideal house; I think I am still sufficiently young to be able to afford to wait."

"You would be so much happier, Edward, if you were married."

"My dear Gisèle, I would do anything to please you; but pray do not ask me to take so serious a step hurriedly. Who tells you that married life would suit me? I feel certain that under the circumstances I would feel most miserable, for I would never remain faithful to a woman I did not love."

"Edward, is it impossible for you to find a woman you could love and to marry her?"

"Quite impossible," he replied, in a tone which was so decisive that the Countess Gisèle felt sure that her worst fears were realised, and that her brother was in love with some actress or ballet-girl or common person, to marry whom would be a mésalliance of the worst kind.

" Edward, you are in love then," she said to him, determined to find out.

" Perhaps, Gisèle ; I think most young officers are. It seems to be the first thing they learn on entering the army."

" I suppose, Edward, all young men have to pass through that stage ; the first pretty face they see makes them believe that they are in love ; young girls also, when they get to be sixteen, frequently feel a flutter and think themselves in love with the first handsome man they meet ; but all that sort of thing is not serious ; it is very like the measles, and generally passes away without leaving any worse effect than a certain sense of foolishness on the part of the person who recovers from such an attack."

" You treat the matter too lightly, Gisèle ; young men may love as seriously as grown-up people. Have you never heard of *Romeo and Juliet?* "

" I hope, my dear Edward, you will take care and not indulge in that kind of violent passion ; there is nothing so dangerous in this world as the love of very young people, for such love is generally carnal and not spiritual, and it never leads to any good."

" Now, my dear Gisèle, do not talk to me as if you were old enough to be my mother. Have you not been in love yourself? Were you not also young enough when you married? So far as I know no evil consequences have arisen from it."

"I married, Edward, because I was advised to marry, and because I liked the husband who was proposed to me : I have since learnt to love him. It is just because marriage has turned out so happily for me that I would also like to see you married."

"It is very kind of you, Gisèle ; but do you not think that if one marriage has succeeded well in a family it is better not to tempt Providence with another? Remember the old proverb that 'the pitcher which goes too often to the well ends by getting broken.' If your married life is happy, it is pretty certain that mine would be the reverse."

"If you start, Edward, with the assumption that your married life will be unhappy, you will no doubt succeed in making it so."

"But why, Gisèle, are you so eager to see me married ?"

"Because I want to see heirs to the Klinkenstein titles and property."

"I suppose you would like me to make a *mariage de convenance*? What a pleasant prospect for me, to be sure ; as long as she had quarterings enough you would be satisfied ; a heraldic marriage is the height of human happiness."

"Do you suppose, Edward, that it is impossible to find a person in your own position in life with whom you could fall in love? A *mariage de convenance* is not exactly what I meant, for I do not ask you to marry any one you do not love ; but I want to impress upon you that when one belongs to a great family one has duties to perform, and that you ought to try and keep up the traditions of the house, for traditions are the precious heirloom of great families, and it is only when children are brought up in them that they become true specimens of what an aristocracy should be, and different from the common people. I do not say that common people are not very good in their way, but I think that when you have given you the inestimable advantage of having been born a nobleman you should not throw it away recklessly ; a true nobleman ought to be in culture and bearing an example to his fellow creatures ; a mésalliance may bring new blood into a family, but it also introduces the vulgarity of its surroundings."

"My dear Gisèle, I have been now some considerable time in Berlin, and I must say that I have not yet come across any aristocratic girls in society with whom I would be at all likely to fall in love, or even to live happily with were I married to one of them."

"Your attention, Edward, was probably directed elsewhere, for I know several young girls who are both pretty and nice."

"Well, Gisèle, is there any one you particularly wish me to marry ? "

"Edward, have you ever thought of Nelly ? "

"Nelly ? Why she is my cousin. What a ridiculous idea."

"Do you think she is not pretty enough ? I know her well, and I assure you she is a charming, sensible girl. She will have a large fortune, which is no drawback ; if you will not give yourself the trouble to make yourself agreeable to her she is of course not likely to fall in love with you."

"My day, Gisèle, is fully occupied. I have no time

to make myself agreeable to her ; besides, I do not want to get married, I have got other things to think about."

"You mean that another woman occupies your thoughts," said the Countess Gisèle, rising from her chair and going up to her brother.

".How do you know ?" replied Count Klinkenstein, taken aback at his sister's direct question.

" I have thought so for a long time," she said ; " I have noticed a change in the tone of your letters since you have been in Berlin."

" Every young man has an ideal love," answered the Count.

" I am afraid, Edward, that she is far from being ideal."

"You cannot expect to find angels in this world," he said, rather sulkily ; " you must take people, and especially women, as they are, and make the best of it."

" Edward," said the Countess Gisèle, putting her arms round his neck, " promise me that you will not marry secretly ; promise that you will tell me before you take the fatal step of marrying beneath you ; we have always been friends, and you know that I wish you well. If you have a mistress, and are in love with her, tell me, and I will do my best to liberate you from her toils, and save you perhaps from committing an act of folly. I know how impetuous you are ; how weak, how kind-hearted, and how easily imposed upon by persons who call themselves your friends. Remember that you are a Klinkenstein ; hold high the banner of the house ; keep your name unsullied, that your children some day may honour you. Be frank

with me : it can only rebound to your advantage.
Promise me what I ask of you. If you have a mistress
I do not ask of you to break with her suddenly, but
try and frequent her society less and less, till it will
become easy for you to separate from her entirely, then
you will be free to enter into a purer union."

Count Klinkenstein thought of his child, and remembered the promise which he had made to Lolo that he
would never marry any one but herself ; he kissed his
sister, and said : " Gisèle, you know how fond I am of
you, and how ready I would be to do almost anything to
please you, but you ask too much. This is not a subject
I very much like to talk to you about ; but this I will
promise you, that I will not marry any one without
first letting you know that I intend to take that step,
and giving you time to persuade me, if you can, not to
take it. I cannot do more than that."

" Very good, Edward," replied the Countess Gisèle,
as she gave her brother a kiss.

As it was no use carrying on the conversation further
Count Klinkenstein left the room, and walked home
in very bad humour, pondering over the possibility of
his one day having to give up his mistress. By chance
he met Sydney Gray in the street, whom he had not
seen for some time.

" How are you getting on, my dear Klinkenstein ? "
said Sydney Gray ; " you seem to be out of sorts.
What is the matter with you ? Anything to do with
your pretty mistress ? "

" To a certain extent Lolo is the cause of it,"
replied the Count, taking his friend's arm and strolling
with him up the street. " My sister has been lecturing

me ; she wants me to give up Lolo, and to get married ; you know how impossible it is for me to do so. She has got some vague idea that I keep a mistress, and by a mistress she means a low woman. Of course I cannot explain everything to her ; besides, I have made promises to Lolo which I must keep."

"It is a bad business," replied Sydney Gray. "I wish you had followed my advice at first, and not allowed yourself to drift into this liaison ; no good will ever come of it."

"Now, Gray, do not say anything nasty about Lolo, for she is such a good girl, and I am still so much in love with her."

"That is just the difficulty of the situation, Klinkenstein ; if Lolo were only a common woman like most other people's mistresses, who generally love every one but the man who keeps them, one might hope to separate you from her. I fully recognise Lolo's charms and merits, and I really believe she loves you, and that is what is so sad about the whole business."

"I am very glad to have your impartial opinion on this point," replied the Count, smiling. "It is very satisfactory to hear other people say that your mistress loves you ; but, Gray, what is done is done, and it is no use worrying oneself now that it is too late to alter matters. Why do you not come more often to see Lolo? She has been asking after you a good deal. It is very wrong to keep away like this without any reason."

"It is not because I do not like her," answered Sydney Gray, "that I abstain from too frequently visiting her house ; I do it because it is painful to see one's friend going to the devil so fast."

"Now steady, Gray," said the Count, bursting out laughing ; "do not be so very hard on me. What have I done to make you think that I am going to the devil, as you so elegantly put it ? "

"You are ruining yourself for that girl," replied Sydney Gray ; " you allow yourself to be imposed upon and pillaged by any one who likes to call himself your friend ; you are growing reckless about everything ; you know that your health is giving way from over excitement, late hours, and what I may call general debauchery ; your indolent good-nature will make you sacrifice anything to avoid worries ; as long as you are amused you are satisfied ; pleasure seems to be now your one aim in life, and in the search after amusements you will allow yourself to forget every duty which is incumbent upon a man of your social position. It seems to me that you have elected to tread the primrose path to the everlasting bonfire ; it may be very pleasant to do so, but it is not noble."

"Everybody seems bent upon lecturing me," exclaimed the Count ; " it is too silly ; my uncle, my sister, and now you can talk to me about nothing but my duties. It seems to me that the first duty of a young officer is to amuse himself ; it is ridiculous to be serious when one is young : I have no turn for that modern invention, the scientific soldier ; I hate study, and I have no intention of becoming a second Moltke ; I can fight when it is necessary to do so, in a good old-fashioned, straightforward way, and when I am not called upon to draw my sword, I mean to make

love to women and to spend my money. You may
call this the primrose way to hell; well I think it is
pleasanter to tread upon flowers, than to worry oneself in climbing up a rugged mountain to gain perhaps
as a reward only a better view of the stars. I do not
care about the stars, and I like the earth."

"I am glad to believe, my dear Klinkenstein, that
you do not mean half you say. If every one professed
the same philosophical views of life as you do, and
carried them out, the world would be a curious place
to live in. By carrying out your idea of amusements,
you are not only ruining yourself, which after all only
affects you, but also the girl you profess to love."

"How?" inquired the Count.

"You surround her with every luxury; you encourage her in every way to spend money; you instil
in her the love of pleasure, ease, and indolence; you
treat her as if she were a hot-house flower; what is
the poor girl to do when you have run through your
money, and she is practically thrown upon the
street?"

"My dear Gray, my estates are large, and there is
still a good margin to borrow upon, so why always
look at the worst side of things; it is foolish to do
so: let us rather look at the bright side of life, and
make the most of it. I am very far from being ruined
as yet; why then contemplate a dreadful future for
Lolo? As long as I possess anything she will share
it with me, and I do not see any probability of my
being ever reduced to such poverty that she will have
to beg for her living."

"I only hope, Klinkenstein, that my fears may

never be realised. However, if you will take the advice of a friend, try and break with Lolo by mutual agreement ; it is the best thing you can do, both for yourself and her."

"You mean to say, Gray, that I should give her a pension, and have done with her ? "

"Yes," replied Sydney Gray.

"Never," answered the Count decisively ; and as they had reached the corner of a street, and their direction lay in opposite ways, they parted without saying anything more.

CHAPTER XXII.

IT was the middle of December, and as the Berlin season does not begin till after the new year, Count Eckstein had informed his nephew that with his permission he would like to spend Christmas at the Castle of Klinkenstein. The castle had been closed ever since its owner had come up to Berlin to join his regiment, and both his sister and the Countess Nelly had expressed a wish to revisit the place which they had not seen for several years. Count Klinkenstein jumped at the idea, as he hoped that in this way he would be rid of his uncle for a short time, and his presence in Berlin always made him feel uneasy. He was rather surprised and disgusted when Count Eckstein one morning informed him that he was also expected to spend the Christmas holidays with the family, and that he would obtain from the military authorities a three weeks' leave of absence for him. There was no possibility of refusing his uncle's request, so Count Klinkenstein reluctantly gave in and promised to come. The morning that this important matter was definitely settled, Count Klinkenstein went to Lolo in very bad humour to pour into her ears all his grievances against his relative who had thus spoilt the *tête-à-tête* they had planned for themselves during the Christmas week. Although it was still pretty early when he reached her house, he found that she was out, and the maid was unable to tell him where she was gone to. There was nothing to do but to wait.

He threw himself upon a couch, and fell into a reverie. His sister had again been advising him to marry, and he felt that if he spent much time in Nelly's company he might very likely fall in love with her, for she was undoubtedly a very pretty girl, sensible and unaffected. He felt that if he were separated from Lolo for the space of three weeks fatal consequences might arise, for what on earth was he to do to pass the time in that dreary Castle of Klinkenstein? He could not be expected to find a solace in the solemn conversation of his uncle; he would be reduced to flirting with Nelly, and from flirtation with a pretty girl it was but one step to falling in love; he knew how weak he was, and how easily influenced by female charms; he began swearing at his uncle and sister, and accused them of having planned a disgraceful trap to catch him, and force him into a marriage with his cousin. If his uncle was really anxious to revisit the Castle of Klinkenstein by all means let him and the rest of the family go there, but there was no reason why he should be forced to follow them; his duty was to stay in Berlin by Lolo's side, and spend Christmas with her. His meditations and the absence of Lolo did not improve his temper; he began asking himself, why was she not at home when he came to see her? He jumped off the couch and stamped about the room, giving the furniture several accidental kicks ; then he sat on the music-stool, and brought his hands londly down upon the key-board of the piano, producing enough noise to rouse the household and making the child in the adjoining room scream ; then he rose in a towering rage, and yelled at the nurse for allowing the infant to make such a noise ; after which he returned into the room, slamming the door behind him, cursing and swearing all the while at things in general, and finally threw himself back upon the couch taking a wicked pleasure in rubbing his dirty boots upon the beautiful silk brocade ; after yawning several times he turned away from the light and made an unsatisfactory attempt to sleep, for as usual he had only gone to bed in the early hours of the morning.

What was Lolo doing meanwhile ?

She was sitting in Ludwig Krause's small studio having her portrait painted. Heinrich Lazarus had spoken to her about his friend the painter, of the difficulties he encountered, and the little encourage-ment he received, so with her usual alacrity to render a service to struggling young artists she at once resolved to have her portrait taken by him. It cannot be said that Ludwig Krause was remarkable for brilliancy of imagination, but he undoubtedly had talent, and he was a hard-working, conscientious artist. She herself had selected the position she was to be taken in and the dress she was to wear, and the portrait which was now nearly finished seemed to be one of the best things Ludwig Krause had so far done.

"I have nearly finished my work," said the painter to his pretty sitter.

"How glad you must be," said Lolo.

"In one sense, I shall be sorry when it is finished, for it is not every day that a poor artist can get a beautiful model to sit to him, and it is certainly very inspiriting to have to paint a pretty face."

"Why is it that you artists must always indulge in compliments ?"

"Perhaps it is because we live in a world of imagination afar from the real world. What sounds an empty compliment to you does not do so to us. We are more often sincere than you give us credit for. Often where the world sees but an ordinary face we perceive it as we should like to paint it ; a face is precious to us, not so much for what it is as for what it can suggest."

"And is my face pretty or merely suggestive ?"

"You would call it flattery if I were to answer that question."

"Never mind, then ; but do your best to make me look pretty, for the portrait is intended as a surprise for Count Klinkenstein."

"Happy man," sighed the painter, as he put a vigorous dash of colour into the picture. He remained silent for some time, then he remarked : "Some people seem to be born lucky, everything goes well with them, while with others nothing succeeds. Look at yourself: a short time ago you were nothing, with poverty staring you in the face ; now you are almost a countess ; you possess a beautiful house, you are surrounded by everything you can desire, and you are living with the man you love."

" It is not all gold that glitters," replied Lolo ; " and though I possess much, and have no right to complain, yet I very much long for the one thing which seems impossible."

" And may I ask what it is ? "

" To be married to Count Klinkenstein."

" Well, well," exclaimed the painter, " who knows that it may not yet come about ?   It is strange that we always sigh for what we have not got, and when we get it we do not very much care about it.   It seems to me, however, that you are very lucky, for if a woman has the artistic temperament it is a great thing for her to be surrounded by luxury, and to be loved, even though it be without the sanction of marriage.   Luxury stimulates the imagination ; how can one paint anything good when one has to live in a garret in a great city ?   If Raphael had not had his Fornarina and the Vatican as his dwelling-place would he have painted his great pictures ?   I think not."

" Why is it that artists generally indulge in illicit love, and are miserable if they marry decently like other people ? " inquired Lolo.

" You must not judge artists by the same moral standard as you would ordinary vulgar people : the commonplace joys of married life may suit the latter ; they would simply kill an artist.   To the true artist who believes in his mission, and who dedicates his life to his work, woman's love is of interest only so far as it facilitates him to present in his works, in an artistic form, the ideas and thoughts which occupy his mind.   When a woman ceases to stimulate his imagination, the artist passes from her to another without painful and unnecessary regrets, just as a bee when it has sucked all the sugar it can obtain from a flower flutters on to seek another."

"It is just because I feel that I may be but a flower, and that some day the bee may fly away, that, though I am surrounded by luxury at present, I do not feel quite happy. Marriage is a security, if not so much for oneself, at least for the children."

"But, supposing you were married to Count Klinkenstein, that would not ensure your happiness, for married people have been known to quarrel, and to run away from each other."

"Do not talk like that," replied Lolo. "Why do you suggest the possibility that Edward would run away from me?"

"Men are more fickle than women," remarked Ludwig Krause.

"If he does, I shall kill myself; that is all."

"I am sure you would do nothing so ridiculous," said the painter, stopping his work for a moment while he squeezed from a tube some fresh colour on to his palette. "Women always talk of killing themselves when they are crossed in love, but they very rarely do it; they cry instead a great deal; it relieves them, and they recover."

"You do not know all women," answered Lolo; "there are some illusions which, if broken, kill. If Edward were to leave me, I assure you I would not survive it. There are deceptions which are unpardonable."

"Well," replied the painter, laughing, "it is hardly worth while discussing the point, as it is not

probable that a man in his senses would abandon so
pretty a woman as yourself once he possessed her,
and if he lost his senses and were to run away you
certainly would not kill yourself for a man who was
evidently mad."

Lolo did not answer, and Ludwig Krause continued
painting in silence. "What is my cousin doing?"
she inquired, after a long pause. "Have you seen
him of late?"

"Oh! he is gone quite mad about politics," replied
the painter, shrugging his shoulders: "he thinks and
dreams of nothing else. He has got wild schemes for
regenerating the world."

"Is there nothing to be done to cure him of this
mania? I would be so thankful to you if you could
find some means of doing it, for I am certain that
if he rushes into politics he will get himself into
trouble; he is so enthusiastic, and so utterly devoid of
common sense."

"I am afraid that it is hopeless to cure him; I have
tried my best, and I have been quite unsuccessful.
There are men who are born to fail in everything they
undertake, and it seems to me that he is one of them."

Lolo thought for a moment, then she said to him:
"Would you like to go to Italy?"

"It is the dream of every young painter to go
there," answered Ludwig Krause with a sigh; "it is
depressing to study Italian art in a museum, and to
feel that it is impossible for one to go and visit the
country where all these works of art were produced.
Some day I hope to get there; but it is not the same
thing to visit Italy when one is old and when one's

illusions are gone, and to see it while one is young and still full of enthusiasm."

" Would you go now if you had the chance ? "

" Certainly," replied the painter ; " I would not hesitate for a moment."

" Then," said Lolo, " I will give you a commission. You know that Venice is the original home of my family ; I am unable to visit it, because Edward cannot get a sufficiently long leave of absence ; the authorities are so niggardly towards young officers in the matter of leave. Well, my intention is to send you there ; you will take my cousin with you, and you will paint sketches for me of Venice and other cities of Italy ; travelling will do Heinrich good, and perhaps cure him of his political craze. I have offered him money before, but he has always refused, so I will give you the money, and you must offer to take him as your companion. Edward allows me heaps of money, so I can afford to pay you well for your sketches ; you must send me plenty of them ; it is a good thing to encourage art when one is rich."

" I accept ! " shouted the painter, dropping his palette, and springing up from his seat to indulge in a wild sort of Indian dance round the small studio. When his feelings had been somewhat relieved by this violent exercise he went up to Lolo, who was in convulsions of laughter, and kissed her hand with effusion.

" You must pardon my strange conduct," he said to her ; " you must remember that it is not every day that a bit of luck comes in the way of a poor and struggling artist. I shall take your cousin with me ; our travelling expenses will not be great, and I hope the journey will cure him of his love for politics. I do not know how to thank you sufficiently for giving me the chance of seeing Italy. I will send you heaps of sketches, for you may be certain that I will not be idle."

" I am very glad that what I propose pleases you," said Lolo, much amused at the way the painter had shown his delight. " You are too excited to-day to continue painting, so we may as well conclude the sitting."

" I do not think that it will be necessary for you to put yourself to the inconvenience of giving me another sitting. The face is quite finished, and I can paint the accessories without troubling you to come here again. What do you think of it ?"

" I am very much pleased with it," remarked Lolo, after looking at the portrait, and it certainly was an excellent likeness ; " but I must go now," she added, looking at her watch ; " it is late, and probably Edward is waiting at home for luncheon."

Ludwig Krause conducted her to the door of the house he inhabited, and helped her to step into the elegant carriage which was waiting for her. As she drove away he waved his hat and shouted a joyous good-bye, then, returning to his studio, he indulged in a further wild dance to let off the exuberance of his joy.

As Lolo entered her drawing-room she was greeted with a yell from Count Klinkenstein, which was something so unusual that it gave her a start.

" Where have you been all this while ?" he shouted

at her. " I have been waiting two hours for you. It is highly inconvenient that you should go out so early."

" You seem to be in a nice humour to-day, Edward," said Lolo, looking at him with astonishment. " What is the matter with you ? "

"The matter with me is that I am in an exceeding bad humour!" roared the Count. "I want you to understand that I do not mean to be kept waiting in this sort of way simply for the convenience of others. Where have you been ? "

"If you had let me know that you would come so early," she replied, very quietly, "I would not have gone out, but would have stayed at home to receive you."

" Indeed ! I am to play second fiddle in this establishment, am I ? It is something new to me. When I want to visit you, I will have to write to you and ask your leave if I may come. Is that what you mean, Lolo? I suppose you will expect me next to knock at your door before coming in, so as to give time to some lover to make his escape?"

" Edward, you are insulting," replied Lolo ; " you have no right to talk to me in that way. I do not believe that you are in your proper senses this morning."

" Where have you been ? " shouted the Count at the top of his voice, and seizing her by the arm. " Are you going to tell me or not ? "

" If it can give you any pleasure to know, Edward, I will tell you. I have spent the morning in the studio of Ludwig Krause, the painter."

" And what were you doing there ? You are like
them all, fickle and unstable ; you still pine after
that immoral Bohemian society in which you were
born and bred ; the society of my brother officers and
myself is, I suppose, too aristocratic and too refined
for you ? It palls on you in the long run ; you
must occasionally go and smell of the gutter from
which you sprang. Confound the painter, and confound your filthy, long-haired cousin. What have
they got to do with you ? You are my mistress,
and I do not intend that any one else shall touch
you."

" Edward, your conduct is unmanly," said Lolo,
looking him straight in the face ; " you knew who I
was when you took me ; you did it with your eyes
open, for I hid nothing from you ; as for your
accusations, they are false, and you know them to be
such." Then she turned her back upon him and went
into her bedroom, closing the door behind her, and
there threw herself upon a couch and burst into tears,
for it was the first time he had spoken a rough word
to her.

This explosion of temper had brought relief to
Count Klinkenstein's ill-humour, and no sooner was
Lolo out of the room than he felt heartily ashamed of
himself, and greatly disgusted at his having hinted
to her that he believed her faithless, when he knew
perfectly well that if there was one man in Berlin
lucky enough to possess a mistress against whom
nothing could be said it was himself. He was afraid
to go into her room, and he did not like the idea of
stealing away from the house without having first

made it up with her. He went to the door of her
bedroom, his hand was on the handle, but he hesitated,
and then his courage failed him, and he turned away.
He cursed at himself; he deplored his brutality to
her; he felt miserable; he swore that if she forgave
him this once he would never use another hard word
to her. What if she were to take him at his word
and become faithless and throw him over? She had
admirers enough, to be sure. The idea of losing her
seemed to him too horrible to bear. Presently he
thought he heard her sobbing in her room; he could
stand it no longer; he opened the door and went in.
Lolo was lying on the couch with her face pressed
against the cushions; he went up quietly, and seating
himself on the edge of the couch, kissed the small
curls of hair in her neck.

"I am sorry for what I said," he murmured to her;
"Lolo, I was in an awfully bad temper when you
came in, and I had been waiting for you for two hours.
I really was not master of my words; I shall never
again say anything nasty to you, and you must forgive
me for this once."

She dried her tears, and throwing her arms round
his neck, kissed him without being able to say a
word.

A little later they were both sitting in the dining-
room having luncheon. Count Klinkenstein was now
in rather high spirits, for he had taken an inhalation
of cocaine to brace up his nerves and to remove the
depression which had followed his outburst of temper.
His health had never been particularly strong, and
late hours and the general fast life he had been

leading since he had **come to** Berlin were beginning to tell upon him, so that of late he had been driven to make use of certain drugs such as cocaine to brace **his** nerves, and chloral to send him to sleep, and he had even contracted a worse habit, for when he felt worried he would have recourse to hypodermic injections of morphia.

"Edward, what made you so angry this morning?" inquired Lolo towards the end of luncheon, when Count Klinkenstein **seemed to have** quite recovered from the **ill** effects **of his outburst of** temper.

"**It was all** due, **Lolo, to that beast of** an uncle of **mine.** Let us drink to his perdition;" and the Count raised a glass full **of wine and** emptied it with **a flourish.**

"**Do not talk in that horrible** way, Edward; what did your uncle **want you to do?** Was it **so** very disagreeable?"

"He is disgustingly selfish, Lolo; **he** wants to score **off me,** but I do not intend to let him do **so. It is** always the **way with aged** relatives; they **want** to treat **us as if we were** children, and had to obey; they cannot mind their own business, and leave other people alone; they must have their fingers in every one's affairs. Confound **the** old General," added the Count between his teeth.

"You are not very explicit in your explanations, Edward."

"My uncle has obtained a three weeks' leave of absence **for me,** Lolo, and now he expects me to go and waste it at Klinkenstein in the company of himself, my sister, and my cousin. Just imagine what a penance for me to have to spend three weeks away from you in their society in that infernal dull place Klinkenstein. I wish the whole castle were at the bottom of the sea."

" Your cousin Nelly will be there ?" inquired Lolo, eagerly.

" Just so, Lolo ; the whole thing is a low, vulgar trick of my uncle, and I will not be taken in by it. They want to get me away from you, Lolo, and to throw me together with Nelly, that I may fall in love with her ; for the long and short of it is, that they want me to marry her, and I do not intend to do it." Then the Count brought down his fist upon the table, making the glasses rattle.

" I thought it would come to that," murmured Lolo, in a low, pathetic voice, which made the Count feel uncomfortable. "She is very pretty, is she not ? "

" Lolo, if she were ten times prettier than yourself, I swear to you that I would not marry her. It is an impossibility. For goodness' sake do not get that idea into your head."

" We are not always masters of ourselves, Edward ; and frequently we drift whither we least expected."

" My uncle is greatly mistaken, if he expects that by taking me down to Klinkenstein he will bring about my marriage with Nelly. It is the very way not to do it. When I am bored to death, and in an infernal bad humour, it is not exactly the moment I select for making love to a girl, however pretty she may be. All my uncle will get by his ingenious, but wicked plan will be, that I shall make myself as nasty and disagreeable as possible all the time I have to remain in his company. He will not try the experiment a second time."

"It is dangerous, however, Edward, to run into temptation," remarked Lolo. "I know how pretty your cousin is, for I have seen her driving with you, and I do not like the idea of your seeing too much of her; men are such weak things when a pretty woman is near them: they catch fire at once like tinder, and then they are ready to do any folly." She brought her chair close to his, and leaning her head against his shoulder, gave him an almost imperceptible kiss, which sent a thrill through him. "Edward," she whispered into his ear, "do not go to Klinkenstein, and do not leave me alone for three weeks."

He felt her hair irritating his cheek; he did not like to look round from fear of being unable to refuse her request, and he remembered that that very morning he had promised the old General that he would obey his orders and follow him to Klinkenstein the next day. It was all very well for him to blackguard his uncle when he was not there, but what would become of Prussian discipline if a junior officer refused to show deference to and obey the orders of his superior? He thought it more prudent not to answer Lolo, and he continued to puff at his cigarette.

"Edward, do not go," he heard her murmur again as she nestled closer to his side. He felt that something resolute must be done, or he would break his word to his uncle, so he pulled himself together and said to her as gently as he could: "Lolo, be a reasonable girl; do not ask from me what is impossible. I have told you already that I have promised my uncle that I would go to Klinkenstein. You would not wish me to break my word, would you? I know I owe you a compensation for abandoning you like this. I ought never to have promised to go down there; but then, my uncle bullied me so about it that at last I gave in, and it is now too late to alter things. I assure you I will slip away as soon as ever I can and return to you, but meanwhile, to soothe you, if there is anything which money can buy, tell me, and it is yours."

" What I want is yourself," replied Lolo, getting up; "and as I cannot have you, I do not want anything else. We women have always to give in to you men." She saw that it was no use worrying him any longer on the subject, so she allowed it to drop.

At that moment a servant entered the room with a note on a silver tray. She opened it; it was from Count Bernstein, an officer in one of the cavalry regiments of the Guards; he invited her and Count Klinkenstein, on behalf of himself and some brother officers, to a big supper that evening which would be given in the most expensive restaurant in Berlin. Several actresses would be there, he said, and they would all be very disappointed if she did not come.

Lolo tossed the note over to Count Klinkenstein. " Read it," she said to him; " what answer do you want me to give to it? For my part I do not feel very much inclined for a rowdy supper to-night."

Count Klinkenstein took the letter and glanced at it. It was just the thing he wanted. After the scene which had taken place that morning, and which had considerably upset his nerves, he felt rather afraid of

being left alone with Lolo ; moreover, it was his last
night before going down to Klinkenstein for three
weeks, and he knew that if he dined *tête-à-tête* with
her she would renew her attempts to dissuade him
from going there. If she persisted long enough he
felt he would yield, and then he foresaw a terrible row
with his uncle, who on the rare occasions when he was
really angry was not a person to be lightly trifled
with. Besides, he wanted constant excitement, **for
he had grown** so accustomed to having it that he felt
quite unwell and **out of** sorts if he was compelled to
pass **a dull evening ; then** with that odious prospect
of having to pass three weeks in the country, and
to live during **that time** what his sister had been
pleased **to call** an **idyllic life, but** which really meant
goody-goody, insipid conversation, and general dulness
from morning **till** night, he thought it absolutely
necessary for his health that he should **take** part that
evening **in** a joyous **rout** which would not break up
till the early hours **of the** morning ; it would brace
up his nerves, and leave him souvenirs **to** dream
about, and so enable him to face, in a **better** frame
of mind, the old General who was waiting for him at
Klinkenstein.

"He is **a** very nice fellow, is this Count Bernstein,"
he began, hesitating a good deal **over** his words, and
speaking very slowly ; "don't you think, Lolo, it would
be very rude of you to refuse without having any real
reason for doing so? We should not hurt people's
feelings unnecessarily. I know him very well, and as
he has no doubt given himself much trouble, and gone
to great expense, to prepare a supper worthy of so

pretty a woman as yourself, we ought not to disappoint him."

"Do as you please," she answered ; " but I must say I would prefer to go to a theatre first, and then to have supper with you alone, for I shall not see you again for so long."

"But, Lolo, there is no objection to our going to a theatre, and as we must sup somewhere afterwards, why not with Count Bernstein ?" She was standing before the looking-glass arranging her hair ; he went up to her, and kissing her ear whispered : " Do accept, Lolo. We shall leave very early and come home, and then we shall be together all night."

"Very good," she replied ; "as it pleases you, Edward, so be it."

She sat down and answered the invitation, accepting it.

CHAPTER XXIII.

IT was a ballet night at the Opera. Count Klinkenstein and his mistress had decided to go there to pass the time before proceeding to Count Bernstein's supper. Lolo was dressed in her best and wore a profusion of diamonds, and as she sat in her box with Count Klinkenstein hid in the background, she attracted all the opera-glasses upon herself, and one of the royal princes was noticed to pay far more attention to her than to what was going on on the stage.

They were giving the old-fashioned and pretty ballet of *Satanella*. It tells the story of a student who has discovered the means of conjuring up a little devil who becomes his slave. One day, however, Satanella appears when the student is out, and rummaging among his books finds the sheet on which the incantation is written by means of which the student has been able to summon him at his pleasure. Satanella promptly burns the sheet, and is henceforth master of the student, who, under the tuition of the little devil, soon falls into bad ways, and is eventually carried off to Hades.

" How I should like to dance like that Italian girl who takes the part of Satanella," said Lolo, turning to the Count.

" You would certainly look very pretty dressed as a little devil," he replied.

" That is the only thing you men ever think about in a ballet. If you are given plenty of good figures scantily clothed, so that they may be seen to advantage, you are quite satisfied. You never consider stage dancing as an art ; you look upon it merely as a pastime for the amusement of men. I know by experience how difficult it is to learn dancing, and what a long training it requires before you can achieve even moderate success in the art."

" I do not want to run down dancing, Lolo, and I quite understand how difficult it must be to learn the technique of the art ; but don't you think that a ballet without a lot of pretty girls with good figures and bright dresses, and without plenty of what we vulgarly call ' legs,' would be a very dull performance ? "

" Certainly not, Edward ; those are merely accessories."

" But very essential ones, Lolo."

" Not at all ; the essential in a good ballet is that the music should be appropriate and refined ; the dancing should be graceful and quiet, not extravagant or rowdy, and it should never be allowed to degenerate into the performance of gymnastical feats simply because they are difficult. The principal artiste should be able to perform the most intricate and difficult steps with perfect ease as if they came to her without an effort, so that the spectators may never become conscious of the pain and anxiety she very likely endures while going through her performance. Moreover, a great *danseuse* must be possessed of a

very mobile face ; for in a form of art in which words
are interdicted all emotions have to be expressed by
the movements of the face and the body, and they
must be so marked that the public may grasp the
situation at a glance.   Pantomime is one of the most
important parts of a ballet-girl's education ; deport-
ment is almost as essential.   But the girl who aspires
to become a really great *danseuse* must not only be
consummate in all the technique of the art, but she
must also be born with the instincts of a tragic
actress, for to stir the emotions of the spectators, as
Taglioni is said to have done, when you are unable to
open your mouth, requires as much genius as to act the
parts of Ophelia or Lady Macbeth.   The ballet, as I
conceive it, should be a picture of all that is most
beautiful and refined ; it should be in turns soothing,
elevating, and inspiriting ; it should for a moment
raise the spectators from the world of vulgar realities
into a world of fantasy ; it should give you a vision of
dreamland—it should be a poem."

  " Lolo, you are quite a manual of the art of dancing.
It is very delightful to listen to you, but what would I
not give to have seen you in the old days prancing
about on the stage of the Victoria Theatre in your
short gauze skirts and pink tights, and putting your
theories of the art into practice."

  " Your mind seems to run on legs, Edward ; you
are very terrestrial ; you have not got much poetry in
you."

  " Lolo, what should a soldier do with poetry ?   It
is a useless encumbrance ; we have to live on the
earth, and make the most of its pleasures.   A soldier

must be practical ; sentiment with him would be out of place, for his chief duty is to destroy. Let us leave sentiment to women, and if they like it let them fill their imaginations with fantastic lovers as a pastime. We officers are not jealous of such lovers, for we know that in the long run you women will still love us coarse soldiers best."

"The world would be terribly dull if we did not sometimes indulge in dreams."

"Dreams ! They are ridiculous things your dreams ; they disturb one's night's rest, and they only appear when one is suffering from indigestion ; I never saw any good in them, Lolo. Give me living, palpitating reality ; that is what I want. It is ten times better than any vision."

"Hold your tongue, Edward, and look at the girl who is dancing now ; does she not give you the impression of ethereal lightness and perfect grace of movement ? "

Count Klinkenstein took his opera-glass, and after looking through them for a time remarked : "She certainly does dance very well. Lolo, is it difficult to make those pirouettes ? "

"Not when you are trained to it, Edward."

"But I suppose it must be very painful at first to go stamping about on the tip of one's toes ? "

"No art can be acquired, Edward, without undergoing much pain and trouble, nor success attained if one lacks energy and perseverance."

The Italian ballerina was in great form that evening, and when the curtain fell a perfect whirlwind of applause rose from the enchanted public, and she had to appear **two** or three times before the curtain to acknowledge her thanks for this public approval.

" What would I not give to be in that girl's place," remarked Lolo **to** the Count ; " what a sensation **of** pleasure it must be to feel that one has the power **to** move a great public like this to enthusiasm and **to know** the intoxication of applause. A moment of applause as she has received to-night must compensate **her for** all the hardship and misery of the life she probably led till she attained to this perfection."

Lolo fell into **a reverie** as she thought of her **own life :** how different it might have been if her father **had lived a little longer ;** how she **might** have become **a** great dancer like **this girl, or** perhaps even better, a great **actress ; with labour and** hard study she might have eventually gained the applause as well as the approbation **of the world ;** fortune had chosen for her the **easy path ; she** had wealth, comfort, all that **women most envy, but** she could never have her ears greeted by **the applause of an** enthusiastic public.

" Lolo, if you are going to indulge in a fit of silence, **I** will **leave you to your** dreams," said the **Count.** " The **entr'acte is long ;** I feel infernally hungry ; these **suppers are** always so very late. I will go and get a nip at the bar ; " and he went out and left her to her meditations.

The ballet was over. Count Klinkenstein and Lolo drove to **the** brilliantly **lit** up restaurant where the supper was **to** take place. Count Bernstein and his brother officers were there to receive them, and they presented Lolo with a beautiful bouquet of flowers. The private rooms where the supper was laid out were furnished in a gaudy style usual in such establishments ; the curtains were of silk, and the chairs and sofas were covered with the same material and heavily gilt ; on the walls there were imitation Gobelin tapestries, representing cupids and wood nymphs, remarkable for the lightness of their attire. Two rooms had been prepared, one as a sitting-room, the other for the supper ; in the latter the table had been decorated with a profusion of flowers, although it was mid-December, but when Count Bernstein undertook to give a supper he was not particular as to what it cost as long as it was smart.

The company consisted of some twelve persons, and besides Lolo a well-known singer from the Opera and two actresses from the Royal Theatre were present. They sat down to supper, where everything which was out of season was served up to them.

"What a pity it is that you have given up the stage," said Count Bernstein, who was seated next to Lolo. " If you had continued on it I am certain you would have attained as much success as some of the ladies here to-night. If I were a girl with as pretty a face as yours I would at once go on the stage, whether I was able to act or not. Facing the public boldly must give one such a sense of independence, and how delightful the applause must be, and for a girl what a pleasure to notice all the opera-glasses turned upon her limbs, of course only for the purpose of admiration, and then such a life opens the door to so many other pleasures besides."

" Well, you are a nice sort of person, Count, to insinuate to me that the chief attraction the stage has for young girls is that it opens the door to their leading an immoral life, or in other words, that it facilitates their coming into contact with you dissolute officers."

" I did not quite mean that," he replied ; " but as your reputation is acknowledged on all sides to be immaculate, we may be allowed to discuss this interesting subject."

" Very well," said Lolo, " and pray, Count, what will you be telling me next, I wonder ? "

" My dear Olga Zanelli," replied Count Bernstein, " before we enter into conversation upon this very delicate ground, let me drink your health to show that we are friends, and that we discuss the subject merely as philosophers would do, who are reputed to have no feelings whatever. Well, you will allow, I think, that if the stage only offered young ladies the prospects of the nunnery it would not attract to itself the girls who were prettiest or most intelligent."

" No one pretends that the stage is a school of morality for actresses, or that it in any way partakes of the nature of a nunnery ; but what I mean to say is, that it is wrong to brand every pretty girl who shows herself on the boards as a person who leads a loose life ; if they do so it is not because they are on the stage, but in spite of it, and if they were engaged in any other profession they would probably do the same."

" That is possible, for it is in the nature of young girls to be naughty, and no confinement in a brazen tower can ensure protection from accidents."

" You are getting horrible, Count."

"Do not be angry, my dear Olga ; you know what a lenient judge an officer is of young ladies who are found in fault. I am the last person who would throw a stone at them."

"I should hope you were," replied Lolo, "for you officers have much to answer for. I have generally found that girls on the stage were naturally a great deal better and more moral than people give them credit for."

"Oh ! indeed !"

"I mean what I say, Count ; but you officers have grown so dissolute and cynical of late that no poor girl, however good her intentions may be, can long escape being exposed to temptation. You prowl about the stage doors ; you follow them as they go home ; you offer them bouquets and invite them to supper, and they, poor things, are often going hungry to bed ! You make love to them with a false sincerity which is very deceptive, and then when they have drunk a great deal of champagne, and are in a state of unusual excitation, you ruin them, and the world thinks you smart, and points its fingers with shame at the girl, and calls her loose and a giddy creature, and condemns the stage as a sink of iniquity."

"We poor officers are such devils," replied the Count, heaving a mock sigh. "Some people would credit us with all the evil in the world ; if we were expelled from Berlin to-morrow what a paradise to be sure the stage would become, and the chorus-girls would remain in a state of such blessed ignorance and insipid innocence that I really think wings would grow upon them as upon cherubim."

" You may not believe it, Count, but I assure you I know many girls on the stage who, in spite of all your temptations, have remained as good and as immaculate as you would wish them to be."

" I do not wish them to be anything of the sort," answered Count Bernstein, laughing ; " but, my dear Olga, without any nonsense, you must confess that if such is the case it is a very rare one indeed. When you have lived half a dozen years or more as an officer of the Guards in a great capital like Berlin, you begin to lose all faith in the absolute morality of even the leading stars at the theatres. Girls do not go on the stage if they are of over sensitive modesty ; prudes are quite out of place there."

" I suppose you would applaud if they all led loose lives ? "

" A loose life is rather a vague term." replied the Count ; " there are so many degrees of chastity."

" I should think you meant of the reverse."

" It does not much matter which way you look at it ; personally I am not a believer in absolute morality, and even your purest nun sometimes allows her imagination to wander away from the straight path."

" You will at least give them credit for succeeding on the whole in restraining their passions. They deserve praise for that."

" Not at all : enforced chastity is not worth a hang."

" Your language, Count, is not choice ; remember you are not in the barrack-rooms."

" I beg your pardon, my dear Olga Zanelli ; I will be more select in my expressions in future, for I would not shock you for anything. But to return to the subject we were discussing so calmly, let me say that I unreservedly consider absolute and enforced chastity a sin, for it is contrary to nature."

"It is a very convenient principle to hold, and certainly you officers do your best to put it into practice."

"And very rightly too. When we make love to actresses and chorus-girls we ought not to be condemned, but rather praised, for we not only amuse ourselves thereby, but all the while we are doing the girls a good turn."

"I should like to know what good you can do them !"

"My dear Olga, you have had some experience of the stage ; do you then really believe that a chorus-girl would be the happier if she took to the stage knowing that neither her modesty would be shocked nor herself exposed to any temptation ; that she would lead a dull and highly respectable life, and might finally some day aspire to enter into the holy state of matrimony with some super of the theatre at which she was engaged ? If such were the prospects of a chorus-girl the morality of the stage might be improved, because all the chorus-girls would be ugly ; you would never get pretty girls to offer themselves for engagement under those conditions."

"Men always talk in that sort of way, because they do not understand us girls. I can assure you that I know many pretty girls who would go on the stage to earn a living, if it afforded them the possibility of leading a respectable and quiet life."

"I doubt it," replied the Count ; "in the class of

society from which chorus-girls are generally recruited I have never heard that there existed a squeamish and exalted idea of the value of chastity. People in that position of life are more natural and less given to idealism."

"The next step will be to openly advocate immorality. It is wonderful what champagne will bring a man to when he has drunk enough of it."

"You misunderstand me. I condemn gross immorality just as I condemn gross chastity; the one is as pernicious and degrading as the other: what I approve of is the half-way house. I would recommend the moderate use of one's senses, and of the good things of this world; we were given senses to cultivate them; let us do so reasonably, and we will get pleasure out of them and not pain, satisfaction and not disgust."

"And who is to decide as to the amount of immorality which is good for us?"

"Every one must of course judge for himself; those who make a mistake are the persons of whom we vulgarly say that they have gone to the devil. Perhaps the best test of the propriety of a man's conduct would be to obtain for it the approval of what the Greek philosophers called the average sane man."

"So, Count, you are learned in the classics, in addition to the great knowledge you possess of the stage?"

"Is it more extraordinary that an officer should have studied the classics, than that a chorus-girl should resemble a vestal virgin?"

"I am sure the girls would beat the officers easily;

but pray, Count, tell me what amount of unchastity would your average sane man recommend to a pretty chorus-girl ? "

"That is a very delicate point indeed. Before deciding one ought to know the person for whom one is prescribing, for people differ so much in tastes and physical development ; what is good for one person may be very poison for another. I should say that a chorus-girl who had a lover and was faithful to him and was deserving of the utmost praise."

" Oh ! " exclaimed Lolo, hiding her face behind her fan. " And if she had more than one lover would she be past redemption ? "

" The propriety of her conduct might certainly be called in question," replied the Count, laughing ; " but I think they are generally satisfied with one at a time, and to change lovers is no worse than for a widow to marry again."

" How comforting ! But all you are saying, Count, is mere chaff ; you do not mean half you say, and I am certain that at the bottom of your heart you admire a woman on the stage who has succeeded in maintaining her good name in the midst of temptation."

" You are mistaken, for I am perfectly sincere in what I say. I maintain, as I have stated before, that absolute chastity in actresses and ballet-girls is an anachronism, and therefore ridiculous. Let the girl who believes in the sanctity of virginity go into a convent, where she can indulge all day in the pitiful struggle to master the rebellion of her passions with which nature thought fit to endow her. Pretty faces

and good forms were given to women to bring joy to
men, and were not intended to be hidden behind
cloisteral walls. Happiness is the end of life, and by
happiness I understand the satisfying of the major
portion of each person's aspirations ; that being so,
consider for a moment what are the aspirations of
the average girl who takes to the stage as a profession.
She is generally drawn from a low class of society ;
her surroundings are mean and vulgar ; the men she
meets are coarse and brutal ; she is very likely a girl
with a highly sensitive nervous temperament ; she
feels vague cravings for refinement and luxury, and
pines to get away from the degrading atmosphere
which surrounds her. For her, under these circumstances, the only door to happiness is the stage door,
and she enters the paradise of the stage, not because
it is a paradise of chastity, but because it opens up to
her the possibility of meeting one of us officers you
would condemn, who will take a fancy to her, make
her happy by surrounding her with wealth and luxury,
enlarge her education, teach her the refined pleasures
of civilisation, and civilisation they say means progress,
and progress, our divines tell us, leads to the higher
morality, whence I infer that the comparative unchastity of such a girl is a higher morality than
would be matrimony coupled with a life spent in the
base atmosphere from which she was drawn, and in
the perpetual company of a howling ruffian. It has
become the fashion nowadays to grow sentimental
over the virtues of the poor, and to decry the immorality of the rich, and especially of us officers. I
will, however, maintain that it is a delusion to suppose

that poverty breeds virtues ; the rich and the poor have
the same natural desires and the same natural longings,
but in the rich they are tempered by refinement, in
the poor they exist in all their pristine bestiality.
The girl whose life would have run in the vicinity of
the gutter is, I am sure, elevated and rendered spirit-
ually better by contact with a well-to-do man of
education, though her relations to him be only those
of a mistress and not of a wife."

"There may be a little truth in what you say,"
remarked Lolo ; "but most of it seems to me to be
merely specious and false ; you leave out of your
count love which purifies many irregular relations ;
where it exists much may be pardoned."

"I grant that, but then you must remember that
there are two kinds of love : the one is but an elegant
term for violent natural desires ; the other, which is
usually much more temperate, and therefore of longer
duration, grows out of habit, hence you will often find
it in existence in the relations which bind a man to
the chorus-girl his mistress."

"Well, Count, you will at least grant that the
superior actresses, who are generally drawn from
better surroundings, may lead respectable lives ; or do
you class them with the poor chorus-girl, and brand
them with the stigma of immorality ? "

"The superior actress more chaste ! " exclaimed
the Count ; "look across the table and judge for
yourself." There was the slightly stout but pretty
opera singer lolling back in her chair in fits of
laughter over an improper story which a young
lieutenant had just been telling her. In one hand she

held an empty champagne glass, which alas! had been filled many a time during the course of the evening, and she was crunching between her white teeth a large chunk of a truffle. That was the singer with the angelic voice who looked so pure and innocent as Marguerite in "Faust."

"No doubt many illusions go when one gives a peep behind the scenes," remarked Lolo, with a sigh; "you must be lenient to them, for they have to undergo many hardships."

"The superior actress may have to undergo many hardships, but she also reaps many rewards. The object of the stage," continued Count Bernstein, "is, as Shakespeare says, to hold as it were the mirror up to nature; to do so effectively one must understand nature as well as life, and, therefore, I conclude that an innocent actress must necessarily mean a bad one. An innocent girl's view of life is a fantastic one; that is why when young girls make their *débuts* as Juliet, Ophelia, or Desdemona, they invariably fail; you must sacrifice your innocence if you want to represent satisfactorily characters like Juliet the rake, Ophelia the prurient-minded, or Desdemona the married fool. To understand the ideal you must have passed, if not through the mill of degradation, at least through the mill of experience."

"What are you discussing so eagerly, Count?" shouted the pretty opera singer across the table to Count Bernstein.

"The morality of the stage," he replied; "we were treating the subject very philosophically."

"The morality of the stage!" she exclaimed; "can

there be a doubt about it ? And you, Count, growing philosophical ? It is too funny." Then she went off into a boisterous fit of laughter.

The champagne had flown pretty freely, and the conversation now became general and noisy ; there was much shouting and clinking of glasses, much chaffing of the waiters ; every moment the stories which were told were getting more and more impossible. In the adjoining room the *tappeur*, who had been hired for the night, was playing selections from Offenbach on the piano.

Supper was over. The company rose, and passed into the other room. Coffee was served and cigarettes were lit, and the officers unbuttoning their tunics stretched themselves out at their ease on the sofas, or rested their legs upon chairs. Lolo sang an Italian song ; one of the actresses gave a recitation ; the opera singer warbled some high notes.

The door opened, and a waiter entered. Addressing Count Bernstein, he said : " Count Immersdorf has sent me to ask whether you would have any objection to his joining your party ? "

" Is he alone ? "

" There is a lady with him," replied the waiter, giving a wink ; " they have been supping together here."

Before Count Bernstein could make any objection, Count Immersdorf appeared at the door with a pretty but vulgar-looking young woman in evening dress.

" My dear Bernstein, you will excuse my bringing Clara Schwartz ; I am sure she can but amuse you all."

Count Bernstein had no choice left but to answer yes.

Clara Schwartz, originally a housemaid, had made her first appearance on the music-hall stage, from which she had passed over to the boards of a theatre dedicated to the production of opera bouffe. She had suddenly acquired a great reputation, and was nightly drawing large houses by the suggestive way in which she sang a particularly improper song. No sooner had she entered the room than she was pressed to go through the performance of her famous ditty. She acceded at once, and after taking a couple of glasses of liqueur to give her courage as she said, she began. A chorus of approval from the officers greeted the termination of her song; an encore was demanded which she did not refuse, and she added several stanzas which the censorship had cut out of the public performance. A young lieutenant with bleary eyes and whose speech was already thick, caught her round the waist in his enthusiasm and kissed her. She took it as a matter of course. It is needless to say that she was very tipsy.

"What a delightful surprise to find you here," remarked Count Immersdorf, as he sat down on the sofa by the side of Lolo. "I see so little of you now, and I should like to see so much. What a difference between a woman like you and a common creature like Clara."

Lolo answered shortly and chiefly in monosyllables, for she hated him, but he would not leave her side. As night wore on, his attentions to Lolo became more marked; he told her of his love, of the ardent passion for her which burnt in his breast and rendered his life miserable. She remained cold and indifferent. At the other end of the room the opera singer was standing by the piano, singing the "King of Thule," and beating time with her ivory fan on the bald head of the *tappeur*, between whose legs there was a bottle of champagne from which he occasionally took a drain to refresh himself.

Suddenly Clara Schwartz, who had been watching Lolo and Count Immersdorf for some time, took off her dainty high-heeled shoe, and hurled it at the Count's head; but her hand was shaky, and she missed her aim; she then rose and made for them, but she was unsteady on her legs, and knocking up against the small table on which the liqueurs had been placed tipped it over. A loud crash followed, and the elegant decanters and glasses lay broken on the floor; a sickly smell of rhum mixed with the odour of various other liqueurs rose from the *débris*. Clara Schwartz, indifferent to the damage she had caused, continued her vacillating course towards Lolo, and having come close enough to her she shook her fist in her face, shouting in her strident and vulgar voice: "Oh! you good-for-nothing creature, you are not satisfied with your rich Count, you want to steal my man too. Do you? You women who loll in luxury are ten times worse than us poor girls. You have nothing to do, and so you are always on the leer for some new man, but you shall not touch mine, do you hear? or you will have to deal with me." Then she shook her fist violently again, and hiccoughed a good deal, and finally addressed a string of epithets at Lolo which

a common woman in the street would have hesitated
to use.

Lolo rose, and going up to Count Klinkenstein, said
to him : " Edward, take me home ; I am not going
to stay here with this woman ; she is drunk."

Count Immersdorf and Clara Schwartz were
wrangling on the sofa.

Count Bernstein helped Lolo to put on her furs,
and when she was ready he offered her his arm, and
led her to the door of the establishment where her
carriage was waiting for her. He apologised for what
had taken place, but she told him that it was not
his fault, for Count Immersdorf had forced his way
into the room.

"And Clara Schwartz," said the Count, as he
handed her into her carriage, "what do you think
of her ? Is she one of those rare and pure creatures
whose defence you took up, and whose presence on
the stage is likely to raise its morality ? "

" Luckily they are not all like her," replied Lolo
laughing, and as she drove away with Count Klinkenstein she waved a good-night to Count Bernstein, for
whom she felt pity because his supper party had been
spoiled through her.

" Charming creature," said Count Bernstein to
himself, as he watched the brougham driving away
down the Linden ; then he remained standing for a
moment on the steps of the restaurant to inhale a
few sniffs of the keen December air before returning
to the smoke-laden atmosphere of the supper-room.

CHAPTER XXIV.

LOLO pulled up the window for it was a cold night and freezing hard, then drawing her furs tightly round her she leant back in the brougham and remained silent.

"What a brute that Clara Schwartz is, to be sure," said Count Klinkenstein.

"Yes," murmured Lolo from under her furs.

"I cannot understand how an educated man like Count Immersdorf can associate with such a creature."

"I do not think he cares much for her," replied Lolo, remembering the passionate declaration of love he had poured into her ear; she gave a little shudder, for she hated Count Immersdorf more than any other man in Berlin, and relapsed into silence. The carriage was skirting the Thiergarten which looked so melancholy in its winter clothing of snow that it had a depressing effect on Lolo's spirits. The recollection of their first quarrel that morning, and of the supper which had terminated in such a disagreeable manner, crossed her mind; she turned to Count Klinkenstein, and remarked: "Everything goes wrong to-day, Edward; I am sure that some one with the evil eye has come across our path."

"Don't talk nonsense, Lolo," was all the answer

she received from the Count, who continued puffing at his cigarette. His thoughts were much more occupied with the unpleasant prospect of having to spend the next three weeks at Klinkenstein with his uncle.

The brougham pulled up at the door of Lolo's abode, and on reaching her apartment she went straight to her bedroom to undress, for she felt tired; the Count, on the other hand, remained some time in the drawing-room, smoking and sipping a brandy-and-soda, for he thought that the abrupt departure from the supper had not allowed him to do sufficient justice to the spirituous drinks. He might have sat there half an hour occupied in thinking how he would spend his time at Klinkenstein, when he pulled out his watch and found that it was 3 a.m. "Lolo must be waiting for me," he said to himself, so he went to his dressing-room and pulled off his things. When he was ready he took a candlestick in his hand and opened the door of her bedroom. She was seated on the bed with her face buried in her hands, and her hair falling loosely upon her shoulders. She did not turn round as he entered the room, and he remained standing for a few moments contemplating the pretty picture before him. A feeling of pride and satisfaction that this charming creature belonged to him passed through the Count's mind as he stood watching his mistress, and if ever he had felt any regrets at the amount of money he had spent on her they certainly did not trouble him at that moment. A bright fire of wooden logs was burning in the grate, and on the night-table a little silver lamp was causing a delicate perfume to evaporate from a water bath. He went and sat down by Lolo on the bed.

"What is the matter with you, Lolo ? " he said to her ; "you seem so sad to-night ? "

"Would you wish me to be merry, Edward, when you are to leave me to-morrow for three weeks ? So far we have never been separated from each other for more than a few days."

He put his arm round her waist and kissed her shoulder. "Lolo, you know I would not leave you unless I were compelled to do so. How can I help myself ? "

"You are a man, Edward, an officer, and yet you are afraid of an old uncle. You are grown-up and independent, and you are the master of your fortune ; you have nothing to expect from your relatives ; do not let your life be governed by their wishes ; do as you please : prove yourself a man, and show your independence. Stay with me. Do not go away."

"It is impossible, Lolo ; my uncle would make such a scene if I threw him over at the last moment."

"So you are more afraid of your uncle than you are of me ! To avoid a scene with him you would not mind making me unhappy. It is not nice of you, Edward. I do everything to please you. I went to this supper to-night only because you wished it, and now, when you might please me so much by staying, you won't."

He felt her foot beating gently against his leg and her body pressing closer against his. She hung down her head, and he felt her hair brushing across his face at every heave of her bosom ; its perfume, and that

which was evaporating from the water bath, seemed
to mount to his head and to excite him incredibly.

"I ought to be more to you than all your family,"
she murmured ; "when people love each other they
do not wish to be separated."

"But, Lolo, I love you more than ever."

"Why, then, will you go away ? " he heard her say.

Never had Lolo appeared to him so fascinating
as at that moment. He had often called her his
treasure, but it seemed to him that he had never
fully realised the value of the treasure he possessed
in her. He began to feel that it was impossible
for him to leave her for three weeks. Why should
he do so merely to satisfy an aged relative ? He
would not do it. Never ! Then a hellish glee seized
him at the idea that his uncle's carefully arranged
plan to throw him together with his cousin with the
object of their marrying each other would come to
nothing. His uncle would be properly punished for
his intrigue.

"Lolo," he said, in a tone which made her look up,
"you shall have your own way. I shall not obey my
uncle, and if he worries me again I will tell him point
blank that I will marry you. I shall not go to Klinkenstein, and my uncle, my sister, and my cousin may
bore themselves to death there all by themselves
during the Christmas holidays. It will serve them
jolly well right."

"You will stay with me ? " said Lolo, astonished at
her success and at the power she still had over him.

"Yes, I will stay with you, Lolo ; or, if you like it
better, we shall make a little journey so as to get

away from Berlin during the three weeks of my leave of absence. I will telegraph to my uncle to-morrow that I cannot come."

"Edward, I would so like to make a journey; I have hardly been out of Berlin in my life."

"I will go anywhere you like; name but the place, Lolo."

"Take me to Paris, Edward."

"Whatever you wish, Lolo, shall be done."

He had yielded. Lolo gave a shout of triumph, and exclaiming, "You shall have your reward," threw her arms tightly round his neck and kissed him with all the ardour and passion of her Southern nature.

It was midday before they were up and dressed. After luncheon Count Klinkenstein went to a telegraph office to compose a telegram to his uncle to explain that he could not come. It was difficult to find a plausible excuse, and after biting the end of the pencil for a considerable time and spoiling several telegraph forms, he gave a violent stamp with his foot which alarmed the clerk in attendance, and leaning upon the desk, wrote quickly a shortly worded missive merely stating that he could not come, without any explanation as to the cause which retained him. He handed the telegram to the clerk, and having paid the fee, left the office greatly relieved at the thought that there was no means of recalling what he had done, and with a higher opinion of his courage because he had at last emancipated himself from the tutelage of his uncle.

As he walked home with a rapid step—for it was freezing hard—he said to himself: "The old General

will probably swear like a trooper on receiving my
telegram ; but what does it matter after all as I will
not hear it ? He was getting too exacting, and it is
about time I put my foot down. He cannot say that
I am mean or ungenerous. I have lent him Klinkenstein ; he may stay there as long as ever he likes ;
and I have given instructions to put all the game in
the preserves at his disposal. Let him burn away all
his ammunition, so long as he leaves me in peace. I
do not see why I should be compelled to bore myself
in his company the very first time I have a holiday of
a few weeks. Youth will not last for ever, nor will
I always have a pretty mistress, so let me make the
most of my time and opportunities. I shall go to
Paris and have a good time of it. I hate Klinkenstein ; it is a dismal hole, and I do not intend to take
up my residence there until they put me into the vault
with my ancestors."

The remainder of the day he was occupied helping
Lolo to select and pack the things which she would
require during her stay in Paris. That evening they
left for Paris by the night express. Lolo, in high
glee at the prospect of seeing the gay French capital,
kept looking out of the window, and saw with much
pleasure the lights of Berlin disappearing in the dark,
while the Count, leaning back in his seat smoking a
cigar, felt a certain satisfaction at the thought that at
that moment his uncle was probably fuming over the
impudence of his nephew.

Count Eckstein was much disturbed on the receipt
of the telegram. He went out into the garden to be
alone and think matters over. No cause was men-

tioned which prevented his nephew from coming ; but the old General, who had also been a young officer once, and knew the world well enough and the rumours of Berlin society, felt at once that the cause was to be sought in that woman of whom he had heard so much, and who was said to be Count Klinkenstein's mistress. He had a strong affection for his nephew, and would sincerely have wished to see his daughter Nelly married to him, especially as he thought that he had noticed a certain liking on her part for her cousin ; but he was quite resolute on one point, and that was that he would never give his consent to the marriage unless he was perfectly assured that his nephew had quite broken off relations with his present mistress. He thought it best not to write to him on the subject for the present ; but he made up his mind to talk very seriously to him on his return to Berlin.

The Countess Nelly was very much annoyed at this sudden resolution of her cousin not to come, as she had looked forward to a pleasant time in his company, and she bored herself all alone in that great castle, never gay at the best of times, but looking doubly dismal when half the rooms were closed and tenantless. There was no other way of spending the day than to stroll about the garden where the snow had been swept away from the main paths, or to sit by the fire of large logs in the stately chimney of the drawing-room reading a book and waiting patiently for the return of the old General, who every day went out into the woods, gun in hand, in search of hares or perhaps an occasional roebuck, and followed by an army of keepers.

Christmas was over, and many a noble German, who had retired into the country to the bosom of his family, began **to emerge** therefrom, and to take a renewed interest in the affairs of this world. The Jockey Club woke up, and its lately deserted rooms became again well filled with a motley crew **of** officers, racing men, and financiers. The quiet and innocent life they had led in the country seemed to have given them a zest for gambling, for by **the** middle of January the Jockey Club was again passing through **one of** its periodical fits of high play. The **ducal head of** the house of Hohenschwanz, **Herr** Schlangenbeck, Count Immersdorf, the rich banker Grunebaum, and several officers, some rich, **most with** but moderate incomes, were well **to the fore. For several** nights **the** gambling was carried **on with great** energy, and when the lull came, it **was found that** several **persons** had been severely hit, **and that there** were not a few victims. Some young officers **had** their debts paid by their families ; Count Immersdorf had also lost a considerable sum, and for **the** next few days he felt very low and sick of **all things.** One young cavalry officer, a Count von Werder, had not only lost all he possessed, but he had **borrowed** largely to be able to continue his high play, with the result that at that moment he was **a ruined** man. Once before, shortly after **he had** joined **his** regiment an inexperienced youth, he had found himself in a similar predicament, but on that occasion he owed a few hundred pounds, whereas now he owed several thousand. The first time his father, an old general, and far from rich, had gone to the Emperor and told him of his son's difficulties, and the aged monarch, as was not unfrequently his wont, had paid the debts of the son of his old servant, but he afterwards sent for the young man, and gave him a severe lecture, telling him that the next time he got into money difficulties he would be turned out of the army. The young Count von Werder, therefore, did not know which way to turn to raise the money he required to meet the debts which he felt himself bound in honour to pay. It was useless to apply to his father, who was poor; he had turned to several of his friends, but they had all declined to help him, for the sum he required was not small, so there appeared nothing left for him to do but to commit suicide. Just as he was on the point of taking this extreme step he thought of Count Klinkenstein. They had both been boys together at the same school in Dresden, and he was aware of Count Klinkenstein's kindness of heart and indifference about money matters; he therefore resolved to telegraph to his schoolfellow, telling him the situation he was in, and asking him for the favour of a loan; if he refused he quite made up his mind to shoot himself. It was therefore with a trembling hand that he went to a telegraph office to compose this telegram of such vital importance to himself, and he allowed it to be seen between the lines that a refusal meant his death warrant.

Count Klinkenstein and Lolo had had a pleasant time of it in Paris. Every night they went to a

theatre or to some other place of amusement; they
lunched and dined in expensive restaurants, and
spent money as if they were the owners of an
endless supply of that commodity. There were
still a few days to run before Count Klinkenstein's
leave was over, and he was dining that evening
with Lolo in a well-known and famous Parisian
restaurant.

"I am getting tired of Paris," she remarked to
her lover; "life is too fast here; one has not got
a moment to oneself; I think we have seen everything which was worth seeing; I am glad we came,
but I shall not be sorry to leave this hotel life,
and to get back to my pretty house in Berlin."

"So will I," he replied. "One finishes by getting
tired of even the best of things; but I must say,
Lolo, we will not dine as well at Berlin as we do
here. That will be one drawback of returning."

"Dining is not the most important event in one's
life, Edward; you men seem to think of nothing
else but your food, and the quality of the wine;
for my part I see little difference between one wine
and another, and I like champagne only on account
of the gas and the pretty foam."

"Women always were barbarians in the matter
of food, Lolo; they have no sense of taste beyond
a liking for sweet things; they eat little, and always
at odd hours of the day, which is very bad for
them; in fact, to put it vulgarly, they have no
guts, and I believe that is the reason why they
are so delicate."

"We women are such dainty things," replied

Lolo, laughing ; "we try to be etherial, and I am sure you would not like us better if we eat like peasants, and grew strong as men. You would not care to see us crunching large lumps of meat ; it must make people who do so so very coarse. You must confess that it is a more pleasing sight to see a pretty woman feed on dainties alone rather than on solid food."

" Well, my dear Lolo, if you can be satisfied with thin air, by all means continue to sip it," said the Count, seating himself by her side on the divan, and giving her a kiss.

A servant knocked at the door of the *cabinet particulier* and entered with a telegram, which he handed to the Count, who took it in a nonchalant manner, and waited several minutes before he opened it, as he was at that moment engaged in conversation with Lolo.

" Is there any answer, Monsieur le Comte ? " inquired the elegant waiter in a respectful voice, but which, nevertheless, showed that he was growing impatient.

Count Klinkenstein tore open the envelope, and began reading. The telegram was worded as follows :—

" MY DEAR FRIEND,—I have got into a difficulty from which I see but little chance of my emerging. Luck has been against me at cards. I owe very large sums which I am, in honour, bound to pay. I have turned to every side for help and found none. I cannot put off for more than a few days the settlement of my accounts. I turn to you

as my last hope, and appeal for help. Save me,
if you can; if you cannot, I will know how to
preserve my honour intact as becomes a Prussian
officer." The telegram was signed, " Werder."

Count Klinkenstein had no sooner run his eye
over it and grasped its contents than he became
deadly pale. He stammered to the waiter to bring
him a telegraph form, and no sooner was he gone
to fetch it than the Count rose in a paroxysm of
nervous excitement, and began walking up and down
the small apartment, muttering incoherent phrases
to himself.

"What is the matter?" asked Lolo, alarmed at
his strange conduct.

"Read the telegram," he said, his voice trembling as he spoke; then he made a great effort, and
shouted to her, " Werder is going to kill himself! "
Then he walked up and down the room with renewed
energy, every now and again stamping on the floor
and making the glasses on the table and the chan-
delier which hung from the ceiling rattle loudly.

Lolo bent down and picked up the telegram which
the Count had thrown on the floor. She read it
attentively, and remained afterwards for a few moments
in meditation. She knew Werder as she knew all
Count Klinkenstein's friends and acquaintances, and
she felt a good deal of sympathy for him, for he was
a good-looking, bright youth, but alas! she was well
aware that he had a character weak as water, and that
he was thoughtless, and in his passion for gambling
capable of perpetrating any folly. She remembered

too that the day she and Count Klinkenstein had left
Berlin so suddenly without informing any of their
acquaintances, Count von Werder had called at her
house, and that he was the only man who knew of
their intention of going to Paris ; he had come to the
station to see them off, and he was the last of her
Berlin friends with whom she had shaken hands. It
gave her a shock to think that on returning to Berlin
she might find that he was dead. She looked up at
Count Klinkenstein, but he did not notice her, for he
was continuing his ambulations with his eyes fixed on
the floor and absorbed in his thoughts.

"Edward," she said, in her low sweet voice, and
then hesitated to go on with what she had intended
to say.

He stopped and looked at her. "Is it not dreadful,
Lolo ? My nerves will not stand this sort of thing ;
the thought that he is going to kill himself acts upon
me like a nightmare."

"Edward, could you not do something to help him ? "

"Something must be done ; but, Lolo, I expect he
owes a very large sum."

"You could pawn my jewels, Edward ; they are
worth a great deal of money, and you might redeem
them slowly whenever you are able."

"Could not think of it," replied the Count ; "besides,
I am certain he owes a great deal more than your
jewels are worth. It would never do for you to be
without jewels ; a pretty woman like you could not
live without them ; she might just as well go about
naked."

"But you must help him," she insisted. "How

foolish it is for men to kill themselves because they owe some money ; how can it possibly save their honour to do so ? "

" Do not irritate me, Lolo ; you do not understand the niceties of our sense of honour. If an officer is fool enough to borrow money, and to give his word of honour that he will repay it, or if he plays at cards on credit and loses, he is bound in honour to meet his liabilities. If he cannot there remains only one thing for him to do, to shoot himself. Werder is quite right ; in his position I would do the same thing."

" But, Edward, what satisfaction can that be to his creditors ? " inquired Lolo, with a look of astonishment.

" Who cares about the creditors ? " said the Count, stopping short and showing considerable irritation. " Who cares about them ? Most probably they are dirty Jews who have enriched themselves on other men's ruin. I am only too glad if they are not paid, but what we officers have to be careful about is our honour. If we have given our promise that we will pay we must do so : whatever happens we must not break our word."

" But, Edward, if you have done your best to pay and you are really unable to do so, have you not done all that can be expected of you, and is it not monstrously wicked to go and kill yourself, for that can do no good to any one ? "

" When an officer is fool enough to play cards on credit he runs the chance of winning money from his adversary ; his adversary, on the other hand, is exposed to having to pay if he loses, and of not being paid if he wins. For this unfair method of play your officer deserves to be punished if luck turns against him ; by killing himself he atones for his fault by showing, as behoves an officer, that he has personal courage, and does not fear death ; therefore in the eyes of his comrades he saves his honour ; but you women will never understand us men, and I am sure that if you loved a man and he had dishonoured himself, instead of turning your back upon him, as you ought to do, you would continue to love him as if nothing had occurred."

"It would depend a great deal on the kind of dishonour he had incurred," replied Lolo ; " I would certainly not cease to love a man simply because he was unable to pay his gambling debts."

The head waiter returned with a bundle of telegraph forms and a pencil ; after laying them down he retired muttering to himself : " There has been a row of some sort ; probably the woman's husband has disturbed the amorous *tête-à-tête* with a telegram. Not the first time I have known this sort of thing happen." Then he went the round of the *cabinets particuliers* to look after the wants of the guests of the establishment.

" What shall I answer ? " said Count Klinkenstein, sitting down and looking at the blank sheet of paper before him. " I have known Werder ever since he was a boy ; we were at school together ; he must not shoot himself. It is scarcely two years ago that Lieutenant von Schmäling committed suicide because he could not pay his gambling debts. I knew him well, and had been playing with him at the Jockey Club the night before he did it. I remember what a shock it gave me when I heard the news. It upset me completely. I could not stand another friend of mine doing the same. My nervous system is not as good as it used to be. I must save Werder at any price, but all the same he is a confounded fool to get into these difficulties." He hesitated for a few moments; then he added slowly: " Lolo, do you not think we have seen everything worth visiting in Paris? Would you be very much annoyed if we went back to Berlin a few days earlier? I cannot do anything for him in Paris; I must be on the spot to help him."

" Let us go back at once," she replied ; " if we delay we may come too late."

" You will not be angry with me for taking you away from Paris so soon, Lolo ? " he said, seating himself by her side.

" Not at all," she answered ; " but telegraph at once to Werder to say that you are coming, and that you will do what you can for him."

Count Klinkenstein did as he was told, and wrote a telegram telling his friend that he was returning at once to Berlin, and begging him not to do anything rash in the meantime.

" We shall leave to-morrow, Lolo," said the Count, ringing the bell for the waiter. When the servant arrived he gave him the telegram to send off and called for his bill. They had intended to go to a theatre, but Lolo preferred to return to the hotel and prepare her boxes, for they had decided to leave early the next morning.

On his arrival in Berlin, Count Klinkenstein at once sent for his friend and inquired into his affairs. He found that he owed between three and four thousand

pounds—a large sum for an impecunious officer to
have run through ; but then, like most young gamblers,
Count von Werder had continued to play when luck
was against him, and he had gone in for that most
fallacious of systems double or quits.

Count Klinkenstein sent for his lawyer, and tele-
graphed for his agent at Dresden to come and meet
him. A consultation then took place as to how the
money was to be raised. The Count was informed
that his affairs were in a very bad way, but he was not
in a humour to pay much attention to any! remon-
strances, and he insisted on the money being found
at once. He was prepared to make sacrifices, and to
accept a high rate of interest, so in a few days the
money was secured and Count von Werder released
from his difficulties. Count Klinkenstein received
from his friend a document in which he promised to
repay the money at the first opportunity, but he knew
perfectly well that such a promise was quite valueless.

The day that this business was settled, Count
Klinkenstein felt as if a great load had fallen off his
shoulders ; he was boisterous and like a boy let out
of school. In the evening Lolo gave a *fête*, and her
pretty house was well filled with visitors. She was
overwhelmed with compliments on her return, and
every one expressed his regrets at her long absence ;
nevertheless her visit to Paris had done her good and
opened her eyes to the world outside Berlin.

CHAPTER XXV.

OLGA ZANELLI had not forgotten her promise to the painter, Ludwig Krause, to supply him with the means of visiting Italy. She had sent the necessary money, and Count Klinkenstein had been informed that it was payment in advance for sketches which were to be supplied to her; he grumbled a good deal at this new extravagance on the part of his mistress, but inwardly he was not sorry when he heard that Lolo's eccentric cousin was to accompany the painter, for without being able to give any particular reason for it he always felt annoyed whenever he ran up against him. Count Klinkenstein would have been pleased if Lolo had had no relations and no terrestrial attachment beyond himself; he would have liked her to have come out of the unknown, like Lohengrin, in a boat drawn by swans.

It was unfortunate that in spite of all the eloquence he used, and all the tact he displayed, the painter failed in his endeavours to persuade Heinrich Lazarus to accompany him on his journey. The enthusiastic youth declined to leave Berlin for the present, but as soon as he had organised and carried out the great political demonstration he contemplated, he promised to follow Ludwig Krause to Italy, and to take a holiday which he much needed.

During the winter months Heinrich Lazarus and Bernard Adler had not been idle. They had been fairly successful in carrying out the programme they had set before themselves, which was to collect together students and other persons interested in politics, and eager to reform the existing state of things, and to unite them into a secret society, whose object it would be to create, when a suitable moment presented itself, a sudden and to the uninitiated apparently a spontaneous demonstration in favour of reform, which would make a deep impression on the public and be much discussed in the press. Heinrich Lazarus was the real soul of the movement; he it was who by his genuine enthusiasm, and his fine-sounding and rhetorical rhapsodies, lured young men to join in this rash enterprise. Bernard Adler was the organiser; he always remained cool in the midst of excitement; he was a keen reader of men's physiognomies; he would watch his opportunities and carefully note the effect of Heinrich's eloquence on the young students who were interested in politics, and who frequently met in the evening to discuss the questions of the day; he would mark down those whom he considered suitable for his purpose, and when an opportune moment presented itself he would talk them over and slowly and very gradually bring them to join the society. It was only by slow degrees, and after the taking of solemn and fantastic oaths of secrecy, that the recruits were finally initiated into the real object of the society. Once in it was difficult if not quite impossible to separate oneself from it. One of the great difficulties that the organisers of this

movement had to contend with was the question of
money, and **it was** again Bernard Adler who came to
the rescue at a critical moment when the society
was **on** the verge of being dissolved from want of
funds to carry out the object it had in view. In
his search for recruits, Bernard Adler had made the
acquaintance of a retired grocer who was well to do,
and at the same time an ardent radical. This individual, Johann Schmalz by name, who had spent the
better half **of his** life behind the counter, suddenly
felt as he approached his fifty-fifth year **a** desire to
immortalise himself. Coarse **and** uneducated as **he
was, he had** lately **taken to studying the** history of
the French Revolution, **and to** reading **the** works of
political economists from those of John Stuart Mill to
the more modern ones of Karl Marx, and the super-
ficial study of such books had so far affected his mind
that he was now quite convinced that he **was called
upon to** regenerate the **world,** and to leave his mark
on the history of his **country.** Bernard Adler had
little difficulty in securing **him** as a recruit to the
society, and a very valuable acquisition he proved to be,
for henceforth the members of the secret association
were able to **hold** their meetings in **a** comfortable
house where **they** were supplied with beer and spirits
gratis by the enthusiastic **retired** tradesman, who
liked to listen to the ravings of these young students
as he sat in his large arm-chair presiding over the
meetings, looking with his dishevelled hair and
flowing **beard like** the picture of an apostle; occasionally, because he thought **that it was in** keeping
with his character, he would break out into prophetic

ravings, which were absolutely devoid of coherence or common sense; nevertheless, his utterances were always received with silence and respect, and he was personally treated with veneration by the young members of the society, for was he not the provider of the satisfying supper and the flowing liquors? However commonplace he might really be, to them at least he was like Zeus, the provider of all good things.

By the beginning of March a sufficient number of recruits had been found to enable the society to make a *coup*. Heinrich Lazarus and Bernard Adler were opposed to any delay, for they found that as a large number of persons had been initiated into the object of the society any unnecessary delay exposed them to the danger of one of their number losing heart and making revelations to the police. It was therefore decided early in the month to make a demonstration against the Government as a protest against the existing state of things, and they had quite made up their minds to face the consequences of their act; but it was true that they did not look forward to receiving a very severe punishment, as they fully expected that their youth and enthusiasm would half excuse any folly they might commit. Still there was a certain satisfaction in being able to look upon oneself as going to face a kind of martyrdom for a cause. It was finally decided that the demonstrations should take place simultaneously at midday in all the principal towns of Germany, on the 22nd of March, the Emperor's birthday, which was kept as a general holiday throughout the country.

As the decisive day approached, Heinrich Lazarus

became very excited. The Sunday morning before
the Emperor's birthday, feeling restless and **not**
knowing what to do with himself, he resolved **to** go
and see his cousin. His visits to her were few and
far between, **for he** always felt oppressed when sitting
in her luxurious apartment, and looking at the woman
which Count Klinkenstein's money had for ever made
it impossible for him to marry. He never left her
house without being conscious **of** an increase **of that**
jealousy against the Count which **was** ever gnawing
at his heart. On this occasion **he** thought that it was
his bounden duty to go and visit Lolo ; he had a
craving to see her again before embarking on this
adventure ; he knew that it might be a leave-taking,
perhaps **for a** long time. **The** future was dark ; of
one thing alone **he was** certain, **that in** a few days he
would **be** lodged **in prison ; what** would happen after-
wards he did **not know ;** he **might** be let off easily or
be condemned to spend a couple of years in a fortress.

As Heinrich was walking down the street meditating **over** his future, **he noticed** ahead the stooping
form **of his** austere father. He stopped dead, not
knowing quite what to do. They had not met since
the row which had taken place between them, after
which Heinrich had been ejected from his father's
house. His first feeling **on** catching sight of his
father **was** to run away and avoid him, but suddenly
he was seized with a sense **of** pride that he had not
succumbed on being abandoned by his parents, but on
the contrary had been able to fight his way unaided
fairly successfully. With head erect, and with his
eyes fixed on his father, he continued his walk. They

were not twenty paces apart when the short-sighted
parson grasped the situation. He stopped short as
if he had been shot, then turning his head away the
Court Chaplain Lazarus sneaked across the road to
avoid meeting his son. With a look of triumph, and
with heart elated by the discomfiture of his father,
Heinrich pursued his course to his cousin's house,
whistling a tune as he went. Lolo was at home, and
received him at once.

"You do not favour me with your visits very often,"
she said to him, pouting her lips as he took a seat by
her side. "Tell me, how are you getting on?"

"Much the same as usual," he replied. "I am still
serving in my bookseller's shop; but I hope soon to
change my position, perhaps for the better, perhaps
for the worse. I have great schemes in my head."

"And what may they be, Heinrich?"

"I cannot tell you for the moment, Lolo; it is a
secret still, but in a few days you will know. I am
tired of serving behind a counter; I feel that the
drudgery of such work is killing me. Better to be in
prison where one has, at least, the time to meditate
than to remain the slave of an ignorant shopkeeper.
I feel aspirations for higher things. I want to
influence my fellow creatures; to better their condition; to show them their power; to develop their
latent energies. The cause I want to espouse is holy,
and I mean to succeed in spite of every difficulty which
lies in my way. I shall soon abandon the petty field
of commerce for the greater and nobler one of politics.
I pine for vaster horizons; the step I am going to
take will release me from thraldom; I will again

breathe freely; I will again feel I am a human creature; whatever noble qualities there may be in me will receive a new impetus, and the depression under which I have laboured will vanish like a mist when the sun shines on it. The decision is irrevocably taken; in a few days I plunge into the stream; the whole course of my life will be changed from that moment; if I sink I can be no worse off than I am at present; if I succeed I will have done some good to my fellow creatures; I will have benefited humanity." He gave vent to several shouts of triumph, and throwing his hat up in the air caught it again as it fell.

"I really think you are quite gone mad, Heinrich, talking such a lot of nonsense. You seem to be in an extraordinary state of excitement to-day. I have never seen you like this before. Do tell me what has happened to you! I am sure it must be something quite extraordinary."

"I have had a good omen, Lolo," he answered, trying to control his emotion. "I have seen my father."

"Oh!" exclaimed Lolo; "and have you been reconciled to him?"

"No," replied Heinrich in a loud voice; "he ran away from me; we shall never be reconciled. I met him in the street to-day while on my way to you; he saw me well enough, and he felt ashamed of himself; he looked the other way and walked across the street to avoid me. When he turned me out of his house he thought that he would starve me into submission; as he had not heard from me for so long he probably thought that I was dead. My sudden appearance before him startled him ; I saw him turn pale ; I knew that he was afraid to meet me ; I saw it in his face ; I looked at him and laughed because of my triumph, for at that moment the old man, in spite of his honours, must have felt that he was a mean cur and a blackguard."

"And the sight of your father running away from you has caused all this excitement ? You are certainly not yourself to-day, Heinrich."

"Do not let us talk of him any more, Lolo ; there are subjects so much more interesting for us to talk about ; he evidently does not care to know either of us ; we can very well do without him ; henceforth let him be dead to us ; we shall never mention his name again."

"He is not worse than lots of others," remarked Lolo.

"It may be so, but we do not know the others whilst we know him. That makes all the difference."

"Have you heard anything of late of your friend the painter ?" inquired Lolo, to change the subject.

"The last letter I had from him was dated Capri ; he calls it a paradise on earth. Happy man who has nothing to restrain him from visiting such beautiful spots, who is free as to his movements, who has no ties to bind him to one place."

"Why don't you go and join him, Heinrich ? There is really nothing which keeps you here, and a journey to Italy would do you so much good."

"It is impossible for the present, Lolo ; all men are not granted the liberty of the artist ; some men have calls which they must fulfil. We cannot foretell the future ; perhaps in six months, perhaps in a year, I may be able to join my friend. The liberty of my movements will depend upon the leniency of others, not on myself."

"You are very mysterious to-day, Heinrich. What on earth is there which can retain you here ? "

"My duty to my country and to my fellow creatures, Lolo."

"You talk as if you were going to be an apostle. I hope you do not propose to go into the streets to preach to people, for if you do so you are sure to get into trouble. Can you not leave politics alone ?"

"No, Lolo ; a man cannot fight against his fate ; he must travel along the course destined for him, whether he likes it or not. I feel I must enter the political arena, although, in all probability, contempt and ridicule, or perhaps even imprisonment await me."

"But, Heinrich, there are already such lots of people engaged in politics ; I am sure they could very well spare you, and you might take up something else which would be more profitable to yourself. You must not run the risk of getting into trouble and being imprisoned. Do you hear, Heinrich ? It would never do ; besides, it must be so very disagreeable to be locked up and deprived of one's liberty."

"When a man is sure of the righteousness of his conduct and of the justice of the cause which he advocates, he is not afraid to face any punishment which may be in store for him ; nay, he will rather court martyrdom, for he will thereby advance rather than retard the triumph of the cause which he has at heart."

"You are quite mad," said Lolo, rather vexed at
the priggish solemnity and foolish eccentricity of her
cousin. "You will do no good to any one by running
your head against a wall. There are plenty of people
whose business it is to govern the country ; let them
look after the interests of the empire ; but for goodness' sake keep quiet and mind your own affairs."

"We will not talk any more about this," replied
Heinrich ; "I do not want to quarrel with you, Lolo,
for you are my best friend. I would like to do so
much for you if I only had the means ; if it could be
possible for me to run away with you, Lolo, and to
begin life far away from our present surroundings, I
would be ready to abandon everything for your sake,
even my desire to enter the political arena, which is to
me more than a desire, for it is a sacred duty." He
paused for a moment, for he felt that he had gone too
far ; then he added, "Perhaps it is as well that it
cannot be, and that I am not exposed to the temptation." He covered his eyes with his hand, and murmured to himself, "What would my friends think if
I fled at the moment of danger?" He rose from
his seat and exclaimed, "They shall never say that
I am as mean as my father."

Lolo remained reclining on the sofa. She had been
startled by what Heinrich had just confessed to her.
Already for some time she had felt that he was in love
with her, and that it had been the reason why he had
abstained from paying too frequent visits to her ; but
she had no conception that he was capable of any
violent passion. Was it his love for her which had
made him so eccentric of late? Did his wild talk

mean that he was meditating some foolish act? She was very fond of her cousin, but she was not in love with him : her love for Count Klinkenstein was still as strong as ever. What was to be done?

For a time there was a dead silence, during which Heinrich felt very foolish, because he had confessed his love to Lolo, and because he felt afraid that he had made himself ridiculous.

"Lolo," he began stammering out, "I hope you will not be angry with me for what I said? We cannot always control our feelings ; I meant to have been silent, so you must pardon me for having spoken. I will never allude to the subject again."

He took her hand and kissed it with sincere, but awkward reverence. "Lolo, I am going away, and probably I shall not see you again for some time. It is perhaps better that it should be so ; but it would give me such pleasure, Lolo, if, during my absence from you, I could possess some keepsake you had given me, and which I would always carry with me."

"Certainly, Heinrich," she replied ; "but mind you are not to keep away for any length of time ; do you hear that? I will not pardon you if you do. Here is my portrait, a miniature on ivory ; will you have it?"

"Lolo, I will always wear it next my heart," he answered dreamily. For a few minutes he remained gazing at it intently, as if he meant to impress every line of the portrait upon his mind ; then, having kissed it, he closed the morocco leather case in which the miniature was set and placed it in his pocket.

They took leave of each other very affectionately, and Lolo, watching him from her window as he went

up the street, with his slouching gait, said to herself:
" Poor fellow ; I really must do something for him ;
it is a pity he is so obstinate ; he is doing no good to
himself here in Berlin. I will send for him in a few
days, and try again to persuade him to go to Italy.
Travelling about the world will open his mind, and
render him more reasonable."

A few evenings later the members of the secret
society met in the house of Johann Schmalz for the
last time before the demonstrations were to take
place, in order to finally settle all the details of that
great event. Johann Schmalz had prepared a more
than usually sumptuous supper to celebrate this
important meeting, and in the corner of the room
were two large barrels of beer, enough to satisfy even
the unquenchable thirst of some five-and-twenty
young students. After three months of talk and
discussion the society was at last going to act.
The members felt that they were becoming persons
of some importance ; in a few days their names and
accounts of their proceedings and political aspirations
would be in every newspaper, and the large body of
socialists in Berlin would no doubt acclaim them as
martyrs to the cause. It was flattering to be made
an idol of, even if the worshippers were only ignorant
workmen advocating socialistic principles.

At the appointed hour some five-and-twenty young
men gathered round the hospitable table of the retired
grocer. There was a feeling of suppressed excitement
in the room, and the students spoke to each other in
mysterious tones and whispers ; they had put on for
that occasion their most serious looks, and they were

trying to look like older men and persons overwhelmed
with the weight of responsibilities. **At** the head of
the table, in his old-fashioned arm-chair of carved
wood, sat Johann Schmalz, their president, with his
hair more dishevelled than usual, and looking as if
he were more than ever impressed with the importance
and dignity of his office.

" There is **a** vacant place," remarked the president
to Heinrich Lazarus ; " who is absent ?"

" Bernard Adler is missing," replied Heinrich ; " but
he will **no doubt** be here directly. He has not been
himself **of late ;** he has grown sullen, and hardly
speaks **to me when I am** with him. I am afraid he
is ill."

" It **would be a** great **blow to** our undertaking,"
remarked the president, " **if so** energetic and capable
an organiser **were to** fail **us at** the last moment. I
almost think that it would be better to put off doing
anything **until** he is himself again. **A** little rest will
do him good ; he has been working too hard."

" On **no** account let **us** put off the demonstrations,"
replied Heinrich ; " everything is ready ; even if
Bernard **is** not capable of taking part in them we
must **go** on with **our** work ; delays never answer ;
every one of us knows what **he has to do ;** the appeal
explaining our principles is already drawn up, and
I will see to **its** being printed secretly by one of
ourselves. We shall **not** get another day this year
so suitable for our purpose as the Emperor's birthday."

" **I look** upon **you as** the soul of the movement,"
said **the** president patronisingly, as he put his hand

on Heinrich's shoulder. "Do what you think is proper; if you decide that the demonstrations can take place without the presence of Bernard Adler, I will give the word of command."

"I am against any delay," said Heinrich.

"It is good," answered the president.

The plan which had been decided upon after a great deal of discussion was that the demonstrations should take place simultaneously in the more important towns of Germany on the Emperor's birthday. On that day at twelve o'clock, when the streets were likely to be most crowded, two members of the society, who would travel to their destination the day before, would go into the most frequented thoroughfares, and distribute copies of a printed appeal to the people to all who passed by. When a sufficient group had been collected round them, they were to address the crowd, and make use of all their eloquence so as to produce a sensation, if possible, before they were stopped by the police. The printed address was carefully worded, and all inflammatory language was avoided. It began by recounting in rather florid language the wrongs of the people, the misery of the working classes, the great burden of the military conscription, and the ever-increasing taxation which was crushing out, not only the energy, but the very life of the people, and making of the citizens of Germany slaves instead of free men. It then condemned strongly the Bismarckian policy, the protective duties which it alleged were ruining the country, the foreign policy of the empire which necessitated the keeping up of so large a standing army, the tyranny of the police, the interference with parliamentary returns which rendered the Reichstag no longer representative of the opinions of the people, and the suppression of the liberty of expression by a servile magistracy, ever ready to lend their help to enforce a high-handed and illegal censorship of the press and of political works. It was also decided that on the eve of the Emperor's birthday the chief members of Radical associations in the different towns would receive a printed anonymous invitation to be present the next day at a certain spot to hear a protest against the government of the country; by this means it was hoped that a favourable audience might be found to listen to the exhortations of the young students. Should the police interfere, the members of the secret society had received instructions to offer no resistance, which would have been quite useless, but to allow themselves to be taken to prison meekly, and such conduct on their part, it was thought, would elicit more expressions of sympathy from the bystanders than if a scuffle were to take place. Thus everything seemed to be arranged, and a line of conduct settled for any emergency which might arise. The prospect of producing a decided sensation seemed bright and promising.

It was getting late. Supper had been partaken of, but the members of the society were still seated round the table, with their mugs of beer more or less full in front of them. Johann Schmalz rose and suggested that on this solemn occasion, when it was probable that they would not meet again for a very long time, Heinrich Lazarus should say a few appropriate words to fire their enthusiasm. The suggestion was greeted with applause, and the president sat down, greatly relieved that he had not been called upon to make a speech, for he felt that he was quite incapable of delivering himself of more than a few dark and oracular sayings.

Heinrich rose to his feet, and remained for a few moments silent, gathering together his ideas and surveying his companions. A feeling of pride rose in him then at the thought that it was his own plan which was about to be carried out, and that it was his enthusiasm and energy which had brought together so many educated young men ready to sacrifice everything with the hope of benefiting their fellow creatures.

" In a few days, my dear friends," he began slowly, " we may be all languishing in prison ; but I can say with pride that I do not think a single one of us shrinks from the ordeal. We are prepared to suffer ; we are prepared to encounter contumely and contempt ; we are prepared to endure injustice at the hands of a bullying and tyrannical police and of a servile magistracy."

A loud chorus of approval followed by the clinking of beer mugs interrupted him. When the tumult had subsided Heinrich continued his speech, and finally worked himself up into a state of delirious enthusiasm.

" We are most of us young men ; our hearts are stout, and we shall not quail, though the journey we are going to undertake is long, and the path steep and dangerous. We shall triumph in the end, though many of us may fall by the way ; blessed will be those who,

though grey haired and broken down with fatigue,
will see after the struggle the dawn of liberty rising in
this beloved country of ours.   We Germans are united
now ; we are strong, but we are not free.   A great
battle had to be fought and great sacrifices endured
to make us a united people ; my dear friends, let us
make ourselves no illusions ; greater sacrifices will
have to be borne, and a more terrible and longer
battle fought before success will smile upon us.
Brute force was required to unite the German race,
to make it homogeneous, to abolish the petty terri-
torial rights of semi-independent princes, last remnants
of an antiquated system ; but to make Germany free,
to crown the work of the Teuton race, to remove the
last traces of the Feudal system, the mark it has left
on the mind of the nation, on its habits, on its methods
of thought, we require not brute force, not the word of
command of the general ready to set in motion his
thousands of soldiers, and to overcome material
obstacles and resistances, but the persuasive power
of speech, the force of example, the untiring energy
in pointing out the way to the higher and nobler
life, the perseverance to ring the gospel of liberty in
the public places and byways of the land, till men
grow accustomed to its sound and learn to appreciate
its nobility.   The glory of the first victory belongs to
the man at arms ; the glory of the second to the apostle
and the martyr ; after the age of the soldier comes the
age of peace ; after the supremacy of material force the
supremacy of the intelligence and of moral power.
Young men, you with the great hearts ; you who have
studied and acquired the learning of the world ; you

who might enter any profession and acquire thereby
social position, distinctions, and material wealth ; you
have preferred to abandon all prospects of gain, and
to sacrifice your lives for the noble cause of elevating
your fellow creatures.   By your eloquence and earnestness you will have to turn away the eyes of the poor
from their degraded surroundings, from the bickerings
and heart burnings of society as at present constituted,
from the oppression under which they groan.   It
will be your task to raise their hearts and drooping
courage ; you will have to sow the seed of aspirations
which will rouse their energies ; you will have to go
into the streets and talk to those who pass ; you will
have to hold up to them the vision of the world as
it might be, not an ideal, not a utopian or impossible
world, but a world where the first duty of a citizen
will not be to train himself to bear arms and to learn
the art of destroying his fellow creatures, but where
the individual man will at least be free, and gross
oppression unknown.   We do not propose to strive
for the impossible ; we point the way to reforms which
can be attained ; we want to regenerate society, not by
bloodshed and crime, but by striving to purify man's
heart, and by appealing to the better qualities which
lie at the bottom of every man's nature.   It is a great
task which you have set yourselves, but you have the
energy of youth in your favour ; your numbers are
small, but your spirits are great ; you are like the
leaven whose bulk, though little, yet is capable of
doing great work ; you will influence and persuade
the persons you come in contact with because your
souls are in your work.   My friends, excuse the short-

comings of the few words I have addressed you on this
solemn occasion, and now let me call on you all to
drink success to the great undertaking on which we
embark in a few days ;—may our beloved country
benefit by our efforts ; some of us will succumb in
the struggle, but some of us, let us hope, will live
long enough to reap the reward of our labours, and
to see the age of the soldier Emperor and of the
iron Chancellor passing away to make room for the
age of peace and fraternity. Hail ! to Germany ; she
has learnt to be great, may she now learn to be free."

They all rose, and with much solemnity emptied
their mugs of beer. Johann Schmalz, overcome by
the eloquence of Heinrich, fell round his neck and
embraced him, an example which was followed by
many others in the room, for these emotional young
men had been sincerely touched by the appeal made
to them.

"This supper," said the president, whose mind was
always running on the history of the French Revo-
tion, "reminds me of the last dinner of the Girondins,"
and as he let himself fall back in his arm-chair overcome with emotion he pulled out his enormous
pocket-handkerchief and wiped away a tear.

CHAPTER XXVI.

IT was getting very late ; the supper had been practically over for some time. Students were collected together in groups, and engaged in loud discussion ; it was evident that the copious flow of beer was beginning to have its effect. The president was engaged with a committee in drawing lots to settle to which town each member of the society was to be sent for the purpose of the demonstrations. Heinrich, who was of a delicate constitution, began to feel unwell at the smell of the victuals and the beer, the pungent odour of herrings and stale salads, and the dense clouds of smoke which filled the room. He rose and taking a chair, sat down by a window which he opened. Leaning out and resting his head against the outside bar, he listened to the confused murmur of voices which came to him from the room. Below was a long, dreary, silent street, poorly lit by a few lamps placed at considerable distances from each other ; at times the belated footsteps of some invisible individual would be heard, gradually dying away in the distance ; above, in the narrow slit between the two long rows of roofs, a bit of dark sky could be seen with a few stars shining through rifts in the clouds. It was March, and the night air, though damp and cold, seemed to do Heinrich good, but gradually it produced a feeling of drowsiness ; he fell into meditations, and slowly and imperceptibly he began to dose.

His thoughts went back to the days of his youth, when he used to play with his cousin Lolo. How often had they not romped about in the fir woods near Berlin, while Pietro Zanelli looked on amused and pleased, encouraging the children in their games, sometimes taking part in them, and helping to play blind-man's-buff under the trees ; and then when they were tired how many stories had he not told them in his vivacious manner, for his long sojourn in Berlin had been unable to alter him, and he remained to the end in thought and manners a perfect Italian. Then he thought of the first beginnings of his boyish love for Lolo ; the many castles in the air he had built as he grew up ; the home he had pictured to himself he would inhabit with her as his wife. Now the boyish love had become a deep passion which agitated his being and made him miserable, and alas ! he knew that his love was not reciprocated. How strangely things had come to pass ! He had always expected that his life would be cast in quiet waters, that he would enter the Church and live his days as a simple parson in some small country town, blessed with the wife he loved and with children growing up around him ; surrounded by his books, perhaps owning as a great luxury a small garden in which he might wander when he wished to meditate, maintaining his simple tastes ; untouched by the turmoil of the world, or the mad struggle permanently going on between men eager alone to attain material wealth and luxury ; leading a quiet and uneventful life, the only landmarks

in which would be domestic events, births, and deaths.
How differently things had come about! Turned
out of his father's house; left to shift for himself;
the vision of the quiet laborious life gone for ever;
thrown by the force of circumstances into the vortex
of political agitation. How would it all end? What
prospects could he look forward to in life? Was
he destined to remain for ever in poverty and obscurity? No! He would work till he forced himself
to the surface; he would become a leader of men;
he would fight against oppression to the end; he
would sacrifice all in the struggle to ameliorate the
position of the working classes. His enthusiasm
and energy wanted an outlet; he would try and
forget his hopeless love for his cousin by accentuat-
ing his love for humanity; he was determined to try
and lead a noble and unselfish life, and be if possible
an example to his fellow creatures. If he could not
win Lolo's love, he could at least try to win her
respect.

From half-dozing meditations he passed over into
the land of dreams. He saw himself in a public place
surrounded by an enormous crowd, who listened in
intense silence to the impassioned words he was
addressing them. As he finished, a wild roar of
applause rose from the dense mass of humanity, loud
as the beating of the billows on a shingly shore. Men
and women were pressing round him; they kissed his
hands and the hem of his garment; they were drunk
with enthusiasm; he had held up to them visions
of the impossible, and they were thankful. He felt
himself lifted from the ground; he was being carried

on men's shoulders. Who could now deny that he was
an orator, a power in the land, a ruler of men by the
mere sound of his voice? At that moment he felt
that he was greater than other men, and he was
overcome with pride. He looked down, and he saw at
his feet a surging throng of thousands ready to obey
his least commands ; he looked up, and there he saw
Lolo at a balcony smiling at his success, waving her
handkerchief and sending him kisses with her hand.
He was overpowered with emotion ; his triumph was
complete ; he could win her love by success.

He awoke with a start, bewildered, and not knowing
for a few moments where he was. Feeling chilly,
he closed the window ; then heaving a sigh that his
dream was over, he rose and returned to the table.
There was much wrangling going on. Lots had been
drawn to decide to which towns each member of the
society was to go, and no one seemed to be satisfied
with the result. They all wanted to be appointed to
Berlin, or to one or two of the other large cities of
Germany. No one wished to be sent to the less
important places ; every one considered his talents too
great to be wasted in demonstrations in minor towns.
Some proposed that a committee should be appointed
to settle the question ; others suggested other pro-
posals. A long and heated discussion ensued. The
president was becoming heartily weary of the business.
It was difficult to maintain order, and it was getting
very late.

" What a pity Bernard Adler is not here," said
Heinrich ; " with his wonderful head for organising he
would arrange matters in a moment."

" Let us send for him," replied the president, " and let there be a truce till he comes."

The proposition met with approval, and Heinrich Lazarus was selected to fetch his friend as quickly as possible. He was putting on his coat and hat to carry out his mission when a ring was heard at the door.

" Here he is ! " shouted several voices, and a young student precipitated himself out of the room to open the door. In a few moments he returned deadly pale, and letting himself fall into a chair, he gasped out : " We are lost ! "

" What is the matter ? " exclaimed every one as they gathered round him.

" You will know in a moment," he replied.

The door opened, and a lieutenant of police, followed by a detachment of men, entered the room ; by his side was Bernard Adler.

When the first moment of surprise was over, Johann Schmalz, making a great effort to overcome the nervousness which had seized him, assumed a theatrical attitude, and addressing himself to the officer said : " I demand of you to explain the meaning of this intrusion into my house at so late an hour of the night ? Are we living under a reign of terror, or is there still liberty in Germany ? Answer me ; what is the object of your coming here ? "

" You will know it directly," replied the officer very calmly ; " I arrest you all in the name of the law. I hope, gentlemen, you will give no trouble, but follow me whither I have instructions to conduct you."

" What are we accused of ? What is our crime ? " asked Johann Schmalz, in a loud voice.

"It is not my business to tell you," replied the officer, very civilly. "Please, sir, make no difficulties; my orders are precise. I have to arrest you all, and to seize every paper I may lay hands upon in the house. You will be so kind as to follow me, for resistance would be useless."

Heinrich Lazarus walked up to Bernard Adler and said to him: "Bernard, what is the meaning of this? Can you explain it? Why did you not come before?"

Bernard Adler, who was looking very pale, turned his eyes away from his friend and avoided answering.

"Bernard, I implore you by our long-standing friendship to tell me what has happened!"

"Well, if you will know it, Heinrich," he replied, with a cynical laugh, "I have saved you all from making fools of yourselves."

"Bernard, have you betrayed us?"

"I have done what I considered most expedient for me to do, nor am I accountable to you for my actions."

"Bernard, you are a blackguard!" shouted Heinrich at his friend; then he stopped short unable on account of his anger to find words sufficiently strong to express the contempt he felt for him.

"It is foolish to make use of foul language," retorted Bernard; "some day you will perhaps be thankful that I saved you from taking part in a series of asinine demonstrations, from which no good could possibly come to any one."

Heinrich did not reply, but turned his back upon the traitor, and overcome with shame that he should ever have been his friend, he went to the furthermost end of the room and, sitting down, covered his face with his hands and wept like a child whose toy has been broken. All his illusions were going, and now the most cherished of all that friendship, which he hoped would last through life, proved false—broken almost before it had begun.

Some of the young hot-headed students, seeing but a small number of police present, tried to break away, but the officer in command merely blew a whistle and a larger force of police appeared. All resistance was soon over. They were ordered to descend into the street, and were there bound together so as to prevent any further attempts at escaping. When the room had been cleared, all the documents on the table were impounded and a search made for others, Bernard Adler leading the way. A couple of men were then left in charge of the apartment, and the lieutenant of police, pleased with his work, marched off with his long detachment of prisoners, guarded by a considerable force of police.

What had happened to lead the police authorities to make this descent on Johann Schmalz's abode that very night, and so to secure at one swoop all the members of the secret society? Who had showed them the way?

Some time before Bernard Adler had made the acquaintance of a rather pretty and intelligent servant girl, engaged in the house of one of the superior police authorities. The acquaintance ripened into a liaison, but unfortunately liaisons cannot be carried on satisfactorily without funds, and Bernard was always suffering from a great dearth of money.

This gave rise to much recrimination between the
two ; she accused him of being an idle, good-for-
nothing fellow, who had not even the means of taking
her out to a music-hall on Sunday nights. He had
grown so infatuated with the girl that in spite of
these quarrels he always returned to her, and finally,
to put an end to the ceaseless disputes, he told her
he was prepared to enter any profession which she
thought would bring him in some money. She
suggested that he should enter the police force ; he
did not like the idea, but she said she would ask
her master to facilitate his entry. He reluctantly
consented to let her act. The next morning, when
she brought her master his breakfast, she boldly
made her request ; he did not like to give her a
blank refusal, for he had not unfrequently taken
liberties with his pretty servant girl, and he knew
that it would be convenient to keep her in good
humour, so he put her off by saying that unless a
man gave some distinct proof of intelligence and
general usefulness he could not be admitted into the
force. She thought over the answer, and when
Bernard next visited her, she told him that he must
do something, otherwise he would not be received.
Bernard replied that he did not quite see what he
could do, but she was not to be denied. She cross-
questioned him as to the life he led, and finally
he confessed he belonged to a secret society. It was
enough. She told him that he must go to her
master and tell him everything, and when he made
objections she threatened to go herself if he did
not. After a long wrangle the matter was settled.

"After all," said Bernard to himself, "whether Heinrich and the others go to prison a few days earlier or a few days later matters very little to them, as go to prison they must, and by confessing the whole business now I may secure for myself a snug berth."

The next morning Bernard Adler presented himself before the police official in question, and on receiving a promise that no hurt would come to him, and an assurance that all that was possible would be done to obtain for him a situation in the detective force, confessed the whole story of his connection with a secret society and betrayed his friends.

That same evening there was a great ball at the French Embassy. All Berlin society was there, and among those present were General Count Eckstein, his daughter the Countess Nelly, and her cousin Count Klinkenstein. After his return from Paris, Count Klinkenstein had carefully avoided his uncle's house, which was only natural, as the first meeting he had had after that episode had not been particularly pleasant. His sister had gone back to Italy directly the Christmas holidays were over, so that Count Klinkenstein had few opportunities of seeing his cousin Nelly except at balls or evening parties.

The old General had been very much annoyed at his nephew's conduct on the occasion of his going to Paris, and when he returned to Berlin, after spending Christmas at Klinkenstein, he began to make diligent inquiries into the life his nephew was leading. The discoveries he made were very distressing to him. He was told of the long-standing liaison with Olga Zanelli, and he found, to his amazement, that in a few years spent in Berlin his nephew had succeeded in seriously damaging his properties by the reckless way in which he had borrowed money. He made up his mind to put a stop to this extravagance by talking to his nephew very seriously, and if he found that words were of no effect he had quite made up his mind to use stronger measures, and to set the machinery of the law in motion, and with the consent of the family demand that his nephew should be placed under *curatel*, that is to say, his estates should be put into the hands of trustees, and only a yearly income be paid to him. Count Eckstein was determined to act with great caution and circumspection, and not to hurry anything, as he still clung to the hope of a marriage between his daughter and her cousin. He was, however, resolved never to consent to such a marriage unless his nephew mended his ways, and unless the liaison with Olga Zanelli were thoroughly and completely broken off and terminated.

The long low ball-room of the French Embassy was hot to suffocation. Although what is known as Berlin court society is not very large, yet that night the crush in the rooms was very great. Every officer who had received an invitation was present, for it was an understood thing in the army that to show that there was no ill feeling among the officers against France such invitations were to be considered commands. Even the old field-marshal, Count von Moltke, who hardly ever went out into society, showed himself that evening.

The band had stopped playing; a hot and thirsty crowd pushed and jostled against each other to escape as soon as possible through the doors of the ball-room, eager to breathe a little fresh air on the staircase, or in the less frequented drawing-rooms. The Countess Nelly, leaning on the arm of Count Klinkenstein, made her way to the furthermost drawing-room, where a window was open, and where there was comparative solitude.

"Let us sit down, Edward," she said to her partner. "I am quite tired of this ball; it is so very hot in that room, and there are too many people here."

"I am quite of your opinion, Nelly," he replied; "it is much more reasonable to sit quietly here than to get oneself into a state of perspiration in the other room. I never very much cared about dancing, and I only indulge in the exercise because it gives one the opportunity of passing one's arms round the waist of a pretty girl."

"Oh!" exclaimed the Countess Nelly, "is it only for that reason that young officers are so eager to dance?"

"I should think that they were mostly of my opinion, Nelly; men generally look fools when they dance, and just imagine how hot we officers must get, hopping about in these tightly buttoned tunics; you women at least have the advantage over us, for you expose a quarter of your bodies to the refreshing breezes. I suppose it is because your natures are hotter than ours that you clothe yourselves so slightly?"

"What is the matter with you to-night, Edward?

All the time we were dancing you did nothing but talk nonsense to me."

The matter with Count Klinkenstein was that he had partaken of a very good dinner, with plenty of wine, and the presence of his cousin Nelly, who was looking particularly pretty that night, excited him to an extraordinary degree. It was very wrong, but alas! such things will occur.

"What is the matter with me?" exclaimed the Count. "The fact is, Nelly, that I am in very high spirits to-night, and as it is so rarely the case, I mean to enjoy myself."

"I suppose you want to convey to me that I bore you, and that you would like to go and amuse yourself elsewhere? By all means go, Edward. I do not want to retain you."

She said this petulantly, and made an attempt to rise, but Count Klinkenstein seized her hand, and pulled her down again on to the seat.

"Nelly, don't go away in a huff; you know perfectly well that I like you much better than the dancing."

"That is very complimentary of you, Edward, as you have just told me you did not care about it at all."

"You are in a nasty humour to-night, Nelly; you twist everything I say into a wrong sense. I want to talk to you reasonably, and you will not listen to me."

"If you have something to say, why do you not come and see me at home? You have not set foot in our house for a very long time."

"Your dreadful sour-tempered father frightens me

away, Nelly; he is always giving me good advice, and generally lecturing me about my conduct, when we meet. I do not feel at all inclined to be good. Don't you think, Nelly, that it is better for us to be naughty when we are young than to begin being so when we are old?"

"Indeed!" exclaimed Nelly, not quite understanding what her cousin meant.

"After all, I am not such a demon," continued Count Klinkenstein, "to entitle my uncle to preach at me as if I were almost past redemption. Every man has his little sins; I love the sight of pretty women. That is not a very dreadful offence, is it, Nelly?"

"Oh no," she replied; "a general love for pretty women must be quite innocent."

"And I have no great admiration, Nelly, for monks and hermits and other persons who renounce the world; I do not approve of their principles of life."

"Everything has its proper place, Edward; you would not wish every man to be an officer, now would you?" she asked, with a smile.

"Certainly not, Nelly; we would never stand everyone being an officer, but every gentleman should be one."

"My father says that young officers are not up to much good nowadays, and that they care more about dissipation than the duties of their profession."

"Your father talks a great deal of nonsense, Nelly; I have no doubt that he was as bad as any of us when he was young."

"Don't talk like that, Edward."

"It is the fashion, Nelly, for old generals to find fault with us young officers. They are jealous of us, because we are capable of enjoying ourselves and because women love us. I would not exchange my present position for that of Field-Marshal Moltke. It seems to me that woman's love is worth more than any field-marshal's baton in the world."

"But that **sort of** thing will not last for ever, Edward. Sooner or later you will get tired of flirting with every pretty young woman you meet."

"Then, Nelly, I suppose I shall have to settle down as they say ; but **I hope the time** is still a long way off when the sight **of a pretty** young woman will have no effect **upon** me."

"Would **it not be** more reasonable to settle down while you are still young, Edward ? "

"**Nelly, you** don't mean to **suggest** to me that **I should go and get married ?** "

"**Why** not, Edward ? "

"**Because it is simply** impossible," he replied, **thinking of his mistress** and his child.

She remained silent for **a time** ; then she asked him why he objected so much to getting married.

"The idea does not suit my temperament, Nelly ; that **is the long and short of it.** I am much **too** flighty **to settle down. I would** probably make a woman miserable **if I** were bound to her for life. I like **my** independence too **much.** Every pretty face I see excites in me a longing to possess it, and such sentiments they say do not conduce **to a** pleasant and happy married life."

"You will change, Edward, **as you** grow older. I

would have thought that it would have been more satisfactory to have loved one woman than to like a great many. Perhaps some day you will fall in love."

Count Klinkenstein gave a sigh. "If I came across a very nice sensible girl, I might perhaps be induced to try the experiment of marriage ; but even if I succeeded in finding her, and were she disposed to accept me, there would still be so many difficulties in the way that I do not think it would come off."

"What hinders you, Edward, from doing as you please? Are you not free?" She said this in a tone of voice which showed such anxiety as to the answer, that he was rather startled and had to ask himself seriously whether it was possible that his cousin was really in love with him and looked forward to the possibility of their being married some day. It took him some time to think how he should turn the question ; but the Countess Nelly, who saw his perplexity, was not to be put off.

"Edward, won't you tell me? You have plenty of money, so you cannot plead poverty as an excuse for not marrying."

"My dear Nelly," he replied, "I have told you already that I am very impressionable, and that the presence of a pretty face makes me feel very queer. It is difficult to discuss the subject of matrimony with so pretty a young lady as yourself, even though we are cousins and are therefore allowed more familiarity in our conversation than if we were strangers."

Nelly blushed, and muttered that he was dreadful.

"Well, I will promise you one thing, Nelly," continued the Count, laughing, "that if ever I do marry it will be no one else but yourself. You see how accommodating I am. As you are so eager to see me married, I leave the matter entirely in your hands, but I do not believe, Nelly, that you will succeed in persuading me to put my neck under the yoke."

A young officer presented himself at that moment and claimed the Countess Nelly as his partner for the next dance. Count Klinkenstein, left to himself, watched them departing arm in arm. "I might do worse than marry her," he said to himself; "she is pretty, intelligent, and has plenty of money. After all, in the end, one must get tired of a mistress however beautiful she may be, and suppers and rowdy parties must sooner or later begin to pall. If ever Lolo gets tired of me, and Nelly is still unmarried, I shall try and make her my wife; but, then, why should Lolo ever tire of me or I of her?"

He stretched himself out on the sofa and remained for some time occupied in laughing to himself over the ridiculous idea of his ever wishing to get rid of his mistress. However, he soon got bored at being left alone, and having sufficiently admired the shepherdesses in the Gobelin tapestry on the opposite wall he rose to take a turn in the ball-room. As he crossed the adjoining apartment he heard two persons discussing together. Looking round he perceived that one of them was his uncle Count Eckstein. He stopped a moment to listen to what they were saying. The old General was explaining to a young officer of the staff the strategy of the battle of Gravelotte. The discovery did not induce Count Klinkenstein to join in the instructive conversation; on the contrary, he escaped as quickly as he could, and finding some congenial companions in the ball-room, he leant against the wall in a quiet corner and discussed with them the last scandal of the day, and that apparently ever-attractive subject to young men—the charms of women and their faithlessness.

The ball was over. A stream of people descended the marble staircase of the Embassy. In the hall ladies wrapped in their furs were talking to young officers while waiting for their carriages. At the door of the house the Suisse of the Embassy, in his gorgeous uniform and cocked hat, gave a loud rap on the floor with his mace as the carriage of an ambassador or of a prince drove up.

"Let us go," said Count Klinkenstein to some young officers who were standing in the hall. "I am walking home; come with me, and we shall have a drink."

They started together to walk along the Unter den Linden. As they approached the corner of the Friedrichstrasse they heard a loud rumour as of men singing, and they saw a large crowd coming towards them.

"What can be the matter?" said Count Klinkenstein to his companions; "let us wait and see."

The crowd approached. In the centre were the twenty-five members of the secret society guarded by police and on their way to prison. They were chanting with great earnestness a revolutionary hymn of melancholy rythm. It had a weird effect in the night with the silent crowd pressing round, and Count Klinkenstein listening to it was visibly touched. He pushed his way through the crowd to get a good view of the prisoners. Heading them was Heinrich Lazarus singing earnestly, with his eyes turned to heaven, ignoring the pushing crowd around, walking as if he were in a dream, and looking like a young saint going to martyrdom. The Count turned away so as not to be seen by his mistress's cousin.

" A lot of socialists going to prison," said one of the young officers, who had inquired of a policeman ; " such creatures ought to be shot ; they are a curse to the country."

Count Klinkenstein did not reply ; he was listening to the chant dying away in the distance.

" Good-night, Klinkenstein," said one of the officers to him ; " if you are going to fall into a reverie we will leave you, for we prefer drinks to sentimental admiration of republican songs."

He replied that he was tired and would go home ; he was glad to be rid of them and to be left alone, for he was boiling over with rage. What business had Lolo's cousin to be a socialist and to let himself fall into the hands of the police ? What would people say when it was discovered that he was indirectly connected with a revolutionist, he an officer in the Gardes du Corps ? It was always the way with mistresses, they were sure to have disreputable relations who brought nothing but trouble and scandal. Would public opinion expect him to throw up Lolo after this ? Then he foresaw more trouble ahead, for what would Lolo do when she would hear to-morrow of the arrest of her disreputable cousin ? In her impetuosity she would probably rush to see him, and expect him

(Count Klinkenstein) to furnish the necessary funds for the defence of this good-for-nothing revolutionary relation of hers.

So thought Count Klinkenstein as he went stamping up his staircase, cursing his mistress and all her connections, and it required the soothing influence of a dose of morphia before his irritated nerves would allow him to fall asleep.

CHAPTER XXVII.

COUNT IMMERSDORF was again in money difficulties. His ill-got money was spent, and he had
lately been losing heavily at cards, but now having
once dipped his hand in crime he had grown reckless
and callous, for he saw no reason why he should not
continue to blackmail society whenever he was in
want of money ; the process seemed so simple, and
had turned out so successfully the first time it had
been tried. There were enough people in Berlin with
a black mark against their characters, and who were
rich enough to pay for silence. He had never before
believed that money could be made so easily, and he
could not help laughing to himself whenever he paid
his aunt the Countess Schnitzel a visit at the gushing
amiability with which she always received him. " It
was so comforting," she used to say, " to have a
nephew upon whom one could depend."

Under these circumstances, instead of worrying
himself how to raise money in a legitimate way, or
dream of committing suicide, Count Immersdorf immediately sent a message to Moses Jacobsohn begging
him to come without delay. Thus it was that towards
dusk on a certain afternoon in the month of March,
Count Immersdorf was waiting in his room for the
ring of the bell which would announce the arrival of

the vendor of old clothes, and ready this time to open the door himself to his disreputable acquaintance, for he had judiciously sent his servant on an errand which would occupy him for a long time and keep him out of the way.

As soon as the Count heard the shuffling steps of the Jew mounting his staircase, he jumped up and was ready at the door to let him in at once.

"Good day, Count," said the Jew, pulling off his greasy cap.

Count Immersdorf answered nothing, but closed the door behind his visitor.

The Jew gave a little laugh as he took a long look at the Count's dismal countenance. "Eh! Count, I hope this time I will not be exposed to the same indignities to which I had to submit the first time I paid you a visit. You noble gentlemen are so strange; one day you scorn us and would kick us out of the house, and the next day you send for us and ask our help."

"Please enter," growled the Count; "we cannot discuss matters in the passage."

"Eh! then you have sent for me again to do a little business for you, Count? Very well! Very well indeed! You will find me most accommodating."

As he spoke Moses Jacobsohn entered the Count's room bowing profusely, and with an irritating look of mock humility upon his face. He walked up to the fireplace, and after selecting an arm-chair with great deliberation sat down in it, and having drawn it close to the fire began warming his hands.

From the other end of the room, Count Immersdorf watched his movements with a certain look of contempt.

"You do not mind my taking a seat, do you, Count? It is a long walk from my poor quarters to your palatial abode, yet I would not like to seat myself before so noble a Count as yourself without leave. Ah! Count, since I have come into contact with our noble aristocracy I have learnt good manners." Moses Jacobsohn threw himself back in his arm-chair and rested his boots on the hob of the grate.

Count Immersdorf did not answer, for he felt at that moment that he could have thrown himself upon his puny visitor and throttled him then and there; but he knew that he required his services, so making a great effort he mastered his ill-humour, and after a short pause, during which he occupied himself walking up and down his room, he felt himself sufficiently calm to reply.

"Make yourself comfortable; put your legs on the table or thrust them into the fire; keep your greasy cap upon your head, if you are afraid of draughts; do what you like. What should I care? When one has dealings with a man like you one is not particular about ceremonial."

"Eh! my dear Count, you have grown quite a philosopher since we last met; you have learnt that true saying that the wise man adapts himself to his company; you have become quite a master in the art of being coarse and insolent; now I feel quite at my ease in your society."

Moses Jacobsohn gave a little laugh, and stretched

his hand out towards a cigar box which lay on the table.

" My dear Count, pray pass me those cigars, or I will have to get up to reach them. I am an inveterate smoker, and I have a very pleasant recollection of your cigars. You are a connoisseur, are your not ? "

Count Immersdorf gave the box a push, and the Jew selected from it the cigar which seemed to him the most promising ; then putting it into his mouth, he struck a match, and having lit it, said to the Count : " My dear Count, I hope you do not object to my smoking here ; you are so very considerate to your guests."

Count Immersdorf was getting very irritated at his visitor's manner. He pretended not to hear the question put to him, and turned his back upon Moses Jacobsohn, who did not seem to mind ; then he took two or three turns up and down his room to give him time to think how he should explain to the Jew what he had on his mind. It was disagreeable to have to begin, but as it had to be done, the sooner it was done the better it would be, so he thought to himself, therefore, suddenly pulling himself up in front of his puny visitor, he leant over him and yelled as he put on a look which was intended to impress Moses Jacobsohn with the fact that he was not to be trifled with : " Do you hear, you confounded Jew ? I want money ; I want money, and money you will have to procure me."

" Tut ! tut ! Count ; you are in want of money ? " replied Moses Jacobsohn undisturbed and continuing to puff at his cigar, while he assumed a look of impudent astonishment at the suggestion conveyed by the Count's words. "You in want of money? Why, you are joking, Count. It is not a year ago that I brought you a very large sum. What has become of it? Already spent? You are indeed an extravagant person!"

"How I spend my money is no business of yours," answered the Count. "I have spent it, and I now require to be furnished with more. It is for you to find the means of doing so."

"You are going too fast, my dear Count; you will come to a bad end if you spend your money at the rate you have been doing. Money cannot be found every day; when we get some we should stick to it, and not throw it away as if we had an endless supply of it at our command. You have been playing cards again; gambling for large stakes, eh! and lost? You have been a fool, Count; let me tell you so; when you see fortune persistently adverse to you you must help her a little, or you will always find yourself in the predicament in which you are at present. If fortune deals out the cards unfairly, the wise man knows how to right the balance."

"I did not send for you to ask your advice, therefore keep it to yourself," retorted Count Immersdorf.

"Do not be alarmed, my dear Count; I do not charge for the advice I give; I present it to you gratis, because I take such an interest in your career."

Count Immersdorf could stand it no more. He walked up to the arm-chair in which his disagreeable visitor was seated, and seizing him by the lappets of his coat gave his frail body a long and vigorous shake, while he shouted: "Do you hear me now, Moses

Jacobsohn ? I will have no more of your infernal impudence. I have sent for you to transact important business with me, and not to play the fool. Will you or will you not pay attention to what I have to say ? If you are not in the humour to transact business to-day, then out you go."

As he finished speaking he gave a last vigorous shake to his prey before letting him loose, and he flattered himself that this high-handed treatment would probably have a salutary effect on the garrulity of the Jew.

Moses Jacobsohn rose from his seat slowly and with great deliberation ; having re-adjusted his coat with an affectation of care he bent down and picked up his well-worn cap, which he had placed on the ground by the side of his chair on entering ; then he blew away the dust which he pretended to discover on it, and after giving it a brush with the sleeve of his coat, put it on. Having cast a glance at the looking-glass over the mantelpiece, and being apparently satisfied with his appearance, he turned round and proceeded with grave and slow steps to retire from the Count's apartment.

When Count Immersdorf saw that the Jew was about to leave the room he shouted to him angrily, feeling all the time a certain kind of admiration for the calmness of the man. " What are you up to now ? Go and sit down again, and learn to behave yourself."

Moses Jacobsohn stopped with one hand on the handle of the door, and replied very quietly, but showing in his tone a certain amount of bitterness:

"Eh! indeed! Am I to be ordered about now? Am I a soldier bound to obey, and you an officer who may command? Am I an individual of no account, who may be insulted with impunity, and you a great person who may lord it as you please? Am I the poor man who may be trampled upon and kicked, and you the plutocrat before whom men must be servile and cringing, because his pockets are full of gold wherewith he can command obedience? Eh! Count, answer me that. Who is rich now, you or I? Who stands in need of help, you or I? Wherefore have I come? Is it for my convenience, or because of your necessity? Who, then, is master of the situation; is it you or I? I think the answer is plain enough, and I know it, and therefore I will brook no insolence from the mouth of an impecunious and broken-down nobleman."

He stopped for breath, while the Count, pale with rage at the cutting remarks of his visitor, muttered in reply: "Jew, you think that you are master here, but you are very much mistaken; and I assure you that if you do not mend your manners, and if you continue to make yourself offensive, I have it in my power to teach you a lesson which you do not expect, and for which you are little prepared."

"You, Count! You, beggarly Count!" shrieked the Jew, this time really losing his temper. "You are prepared to teach me anything, are you? You are prepared to teach nothing but how to cheat at cards and how to swindle your neighbour. Count Immersdorf, you are taking to threats now, last resource of the coward; very well, let me tell you, then,

that I am not afraid of you. Do your worst ; do your
very worst : all your threats are mere idle words."

"We shall see that, you filthy Jew!" roared the
Count, shaking his fist at his antagonist. "I have but
to say a word to the police and you will spend the
remainder of your days in prison."

Moses Jacobsohn let go the handle of the door and
leaning against the wall, for he looked as if he required
support, remained for some time with his mouth open
unable to speak, so overcome was he by what he
considered the brazen-faced impudence of the Count.
When he had somewhat recovered his self-possession,
he replied, dropping the chaffing tone he had assumed
at first, and showing in his voice the bitter hatred he
felt for his aristocratic partner in crime.

"You are going to turn informer now, Count? Eh!
You, the aristocratic gentleman, not satisfied with
taking part in crimes and profiting largely by them,
would now become a hireling of the police, and earn
a little money by betraying others. Let me tell you,
Count, that you are a very contemptible creature ; you
can bully and bluster and threaten a great deal, but
if you reflected for a moment you would see that
you are powerless and unable to do me any harm.
Supposing you went to the police and denounced me,
do you suppose that they would easily believe your
story? No, not unless you supplied them with facts,
proofs, witnesses ; that is to say, that of your own
free will you would have to confess before the world
your crimes, your turpitude, your connection with low
blackguards like myself. If you then received a
free pardon as a reward for your honourable conduct,

in what position would you find yourself? You, the
Count bearing an honoured name—you, the member
of the Jockey Club, the gambler, the seducer of other
men's wives, the dishonest spendthrift—you, the man
accustomed to luxuries—where would you find yourself
on the morrow of your confession? Hunted from
society, shunned by honest men and blackguards alike,
pointed at by the finger of scorn, contemptible in the
eyes of all, what a blessed lot yours would be indeed?
What would become of you, you who do not possess
a penny in the world? Why you would sink to the
level of the gutter, and die of hunger in a hovel.
Denounce me, and I shall be revenged indeed. Denounce me? Count, you lie when you say so, for
you dare not do it."

Moses Jacobsohn paused for a moment to recover
breath, then he began speaking again, while Count
Immersdorf remained standing as if he were petri-
fied, feeling that what was being said to him was
perfectly true.

" You talk of denouncing, well let me tell you,
Count, of us two I am the only one who can do so.
I have nothing to lose, no social position, and my
associates would not turn their backs upon me if I
did it ; I would no more starve afterwards than before,
and your honest man would pity me, and say that
my poverty had driven me into crime. You see
how our cases differ. If I went to the police with
a penitent face, and declared I was sorry for my evil
ways, and ready to make disclosures, I would not
only be listened to, but I would probably get the
promise of an imperial pardon. They would think

it natural of me that I should be acquainted with
crime ; they would not believe it possible of you."

The door had already been half opened by Moses
Jacobsohn. Count Immersdorf went and closed it ;
then putting his hand on the Jew's back he pushed
him gently towards the arm-chair in which he had
previously sat.

"Go and sit down again," he said to him, with a
softened voice, for he felt that it was no use struggling
with his puny, but dangerous antagonist. "Let us
make peace. It is foolish of us to quarrel. Go ; sit
down, and let us talk business."

The Jew obeyed ; he walked slowly back to his
arm-chair satisfied with his triumph ; then striking a
match he re-lit his cigar which had gone out, and
having stretched himself, said : "Now, Count, tell me
quickly what you want ; so far you have been but
wasting my time."

"I have already told you that I want money ; I want
it very badly ; find me the means of procuring some."

"That is no easy matter," remarked the Jew ;
"you seem to think that because I belong to a
hardworking and industrious race, therefore I must
always have money at my command, or at least the
means of procuring some. My dear Count, money
is scarce for men of all races and creeds, and will
not come when you whistle for it. You had a fair
amount recently in your possession ; had you been
wise you would have made it go a longer way than
you have done."

"Money was meant to be spent," said the Count ;
"I do not admire misers."

" Nor I spendthrifts," replied the Jew.

Count Immersdorf remained silent for a few minutes not knowing quite what to suggest. Suddenly a bright idea struck him. Perhaps the Jew had not spent his portion of the money won by their criminal operations.

" Moses Jacobsohn, have you got any money ? " said the Count in a soft and winning voice, as if he were the best friend in the world of the little Jew. " If you have, you might lend me some, and I would repay it to you as soon as possible. Of course I am quite prepared to give you good interest on it."

" My dear Count," answered the Jew ; " do you take me for a fool ? What money I have been able to make, toiling hard, saving one penny after another, I mean to keep ; or if I invest it, it will be where the investment appears likely to turn up profitable to myself. I will not easily risk losing what I have gained with so much difficulty."

" What has become of your share of the money we received ? "

" It is invested in safe hands, my dear Count, and there it will remain for the present. We Jews help each other ; my money is lent to men of my creed whose word I can trust, who will return it to me when I want it, and who punctually fulfil their obligations to me in the matter of interest. My peace of mind would not be increased by knowing that my savings were in your keeping, though you gave me a thousand bonds duly signed and sealed, that you would repay them to me when called upon. Let us talk no more of this."

" Well, then, if you will not lend me any money, perhaps you will be accommodating enough to win some by the same process we employed before with so much success."

" There is an adage," remarked the Jew, " that 'the pot which goes too often to the well ends by getting broken.' "

" That may be very true," replied the Count, " but it does not apply to our case. We have only raised money by sending threatening letters once ; we can very well try the same process a second time. Remember how easily it was done, and how well it answered."

" My dear Count, you are so eager to clutch hold of money that you refuse to see any difficulties ahead ; but I must remark to you that what succeeded then need not succeed now, and that I am not at the present moment in the same position in which I was when I volunteered to visit you on my own account."

" What has happened to change things ?" inquired the Count, rather alarmed. " Have the police been informed of anything ? "

" No ; they are no more intelligent than they used to be, but I have lost my associates."

" What has become of them ? "

" They are gone to America ; they are safer there than here, and having a little capital they have prospects of bettering themselves."

" That is no doubt very awkward," remarked the Count ; " but, nevertheless, we two can make a bold stroke by ourselves without the help of others."

" It is a question whether it is worth my while to

run the risk ; when I have wound up my affairs here
I mean to follow the example of my friends, and
to say good-bye to the fatherland. The police are
getting too troublesome for me. It is true that I
should like to earn a little more money, and to
increase my small capital ; all the same, I would not
like to be caught at the last moment, and instead
of enjoying the boasted freedom of America to be
compelled to spend the next ten years of my life in
a German prison. It is not an agreeable prospect
to look forward to at my age. Yet the more money
one has the better it is ; one wants it badly over
there if one wishes to succeed, and it is a pleasant
thought to indulge in that some day I may return
to Berlin a millionaire, and be asked to dinner by
the great people."

. "It is a noble ambition," remarked the Count ;
"but to satisfy it you must remember never to let
a chance of making money go by. If you lack
courage you will never succeed. Bear that in mind."

"Very good advice," said the Jew, giving a little
laugh ; "but I can cap it : ' Be rash, and you will
break your neck.' "

"My good fellow," replied the Count, affecting to
be amused at what the Jew had said, but feeling
really very irritated at the difficulties he was making,
" what can we want more than two resolute persons
for the work we have in hand ? I will point out the
individual who is to be blackmailed ; I will write
the threatening letter, you will deliver it and collect
the ransom. The whole thing is mere child's play ;
the fewer we are the more secret we can keep our

plans ; we shall divide the spoil between us ; what can be fairer than that ? "

" It is very easy to write the letter and to deliver it ; the danger comes in, my dear Count, when you have to collect the spoil ; and then, you are not sure that while it is being put into your hands a detective will not spring upon you and run you in. One pauses before unseen dangers."

" You were not so timid on a former occasion."

" On a former occasion the danger was less, for it was equally distributed amongst my associates ; one of us might have been caught, it was hardly likely that we should all be so ; moreover, the unfortunate one knew that when he came out of prison he would receive his share of whatever spoil had been collected. Now I am alone ; if we issue four threatening letters, I run four chances of being caught in receiving the ransom. This increase of danger makes one think twice whether it is worth one's while to incur it lightly."

" Think of all you will be able to do with your share of the money ; a little capital is a great lever in the hands of an energetic man like yourself ; with a little money in America you can rise quickly ; you may become a millionaire ; you may return, and be made a baron by the Emperor."

" That is the only reason," replied Moses Jacobsohn, with much sincerity, " which would induce me to embark again on so dangerous a venture."

" You have lost your nerve," remarked the Count, getting irritated at the long delay in arranging matters. " Will you or will you not undertake one more stroke of business with me. It is getting late; I am tired of beating round the bush. If you will not help me you had better go, for your further presence here only tends to irritate me."

Moses Jacobsohn did not answer, but remained thinking the matter over in his head.

"For God's sake, give me a plain answer," muttered the Count, beginning again to pace his room as if that exercise would soothe his nerves. "I must have the money; if I cannot get it with you, then I must set to work to get it alone."

"Have you at least got a promising subject?" inquired the Jew.

"Certainly; any number," replied the Count with eagerness, for he thought that the question showed that his visitor was about to yield to the temptation offered him of making some money.

"Well, my dear Count," said the Jew, after another moment's deliberation, "I will venture once more into the business; but, mind you, only once more, and I must further insist on your issuing only one threatening letter at a time; we must act slowly, and with caution."

"Very good," answered Count Immersdorf: "I am ready to do anything you like, so long as I get money. Is there anything else you would like to suggest?"

"Yes," replied Moses Jacobsohn, "the first threatening letter we issue this time should be sent to the person on your list who is least likely to make difficulties about paying, and as women are more easily frightened than men I would suggest that our first letter be sent to a woman."

" As you please," said the Count ; " as it is, I have a woman in view."

" Who is she ? "

" The mistress of Count Klinkenstein."

" What has she done ? "

" Been faithful to him, the silly fool ! " replied the Count, feeling bitterly the humiliation that his efforts to win her love had so far not met with success.

" Do you propose to accuse her of that ? "

" No, we shall threaten to inform Count Klinkenstein that his mistress has been faithless to him, unless she gives us substantial hush money. There is nothing easier than to make a man believe that his mistress is faithless to him, especially when he loves her. She will pay rather than run the risk of breaking with him. Where would she find another man who would spend the same amount of money upon her which he does ? "

" Your proposal seems very reasonable," remarked the Jew ; " women kept by rich men are usually not particular about the money they spend. Do you know her, Count ? "

" Very well."

" What sort of a person is she ? "

" An obstinate, foolish woman, and a great spend-thrift. Only look at the way she lives."

" Shall we ask her for £1,000 ? "

" That is the very least," exclaimed the Count ; " let her sell her jewels, if she wants to save her reputation."

" My dear Count," said the Jew, " let us be steady. It is wiser to ask several persons for small contributions which they can easily afford to give, than to squeeze from one person a large sum which he will only part from with difficulty, and the obtaining of which increases the risks which we have to run."

"Very well, let it be only a paltry £1,000," answered the Count, who saw the wisdom of the Jew's advice, but who nevertheless felt annoyed that the first letter would only bring him in as his share the insignificant sum of £500.

"Will you write the letter now?" asked Moses Jacobsohn.

"No, I am tired: I will compose it later at my leisure; it will take me some time to word it properly. A great deal of the effect lies in the wording, so I must spend some care on it. By the way, tell me, how shall the money be paid?"

"Let her send it in banknotes to this address," said the Jew, taking up a pencil which lay on the table, and writing a name on a piece of paper. "You see it is not my proper name, but one I assume when I wish to receive compromising letters; and the address is that of a friend of mine who keeps a barber's shop. If the police come down on him, he declares he does not know for which of his clients it is intended, and he warns me not to ask for the letter. You see the trick is very simple."

Count Immersdorf folded the paper, and put it away carefully into his pocket book.

Moses Jacobsohn rose from his seat, and said: "My dear Count, I think this business is now settled to your satisfaction, and so I will not trouble you further with the pleasure of my society."

" Do not hurry away," replied the Count, quite politely ; " now we begin to understand each other we may become very good friends indeed. Please take another cigar to keep you going on your walk home ; it is a long way to your shop."

" Thank you," replied the Jew, as he put one of the Count's excellent cigars into his pocket, " I never refuse a request so civilly worded. Good-bye, my dear Count ; good-bye."

Count Immersdorf accompanied his visitor to the door, where, after the exchange of several exaggerated bows and salutations, they took leave of each other with every token of regard and esteem, but no sooner was the outer door of the apartment closed than he gave relief to his feelings by a volley of oaths and foul epithets all to the address of the retiring Jew. Then he entered his dressing-room, and got ready to dine at the Jockey Club.

CHAPTER XXVIII.

THE morning after the ball at the French Embassy, Count Klinkenstein rose early, having had a sleepless night. He immediately sent out his servant to buy as many different newspapers as he could find, for he was anxious to see what would be said about the arrest of Heinrich Lazarus and his associates. He was afraid that his name might appear in connection with that affair, for he was certain that sooner or later some enterprising journalist would discover the connection between Lolo and one of these confounded socialists, and he knew that it would give rise to innumerable bad jokes and disagreeable allusions in the press.

When the newspapers were brought to him, he glanced through them hurriedly; there were endless columns giving accounts of the French ball, the names of the persons present, and descriptions of the ladies' dresses, but not a word about what interested him most; all he was able to discover, after a long search, was a hidden paragraph in one of the papers, merely stating that some anarchists had been arrested the previous night by the police and taken to prison. He felt rather relieved at that.

"I will go to Lolo at once," he said to himself, throwing off his dressing-gown and preparing to put on his uniform; "and I will tell her to be very discreet in what she does, so as not to draw attention to the fact that she is connected in any way with these revolutionists. As for that confounded cousin of hers, he must now shift for himself."

As soon as he was ready he went out, and hailing a cab ordered it to drive to the house of his mistress. It was still very early when he got there, and bursting into Lolo's apartment he found her still in bed. She was startled by this sudden and unexpected intrusion at that early hour.

"What is the matter, Edward?" she exclaimed, casting aside the bed-clothes with the intention of getting up at once to throw herself into his arms.

"Don't be alarmed, Lolo; nothing very serious has happened, except that your confounded cousin has got himself into trouble."

"What has he done?" she cried, slipping out of the great state bed and going up to Count Klinkenstein.

"The police have got hold of him, Lolo; and you may be pretty sure they will not let him go so very easily."

"They have made a mistake, Edward. Do you know what they accuse him of?"

"Do not trouble yourself any further about him, Lolo. He has become a socialist; do you hear, a confounded socialist? A good Government like ours should knock such vermin on the head and extirpate them completely."

"I thought it would end like that," she said; "even as a boy he had such wild unpractical ideas;

but I am sure that he did not mean any harm. What will they do with him, Edward? Do you know?"

"They will lock him up in prison for a long period instead of cutting off his head, as they ought to do."

"Do not talk like that, Edward; we must save him somehow. Can we not get him out of the country?"

"You are mad, Lolo. Am I an officer in the Gardes du Corps to help a criminal to escape? You do not know what you are talking about."

"He is not a criminal; he has only been foolish."

"Not a criminal when he has plotted against the State? It is the worst of all crimes, and quite unpardonable."

"You are cruel," she said, turning away, and seating herself on the side of the bed. "I suppose it is in the nature of officers to be so."

"Now, Lolo," replied the Count, somewhat angrily, "I won't have you do anything foolish. Your cousin has gone to the bad, and therefore the sooner you forget his existence the better it will be."

She remained silent for a few minutes, thinking over in her mind what would be the best way to help her unfortunate relative; then she rang the bell for her maid.

Count Klinkenstein looked at her, wondering what would come next. He saw she had arrived at some decision, and he wished to know what it was.

"Lolo, what are you going to do now?" he said to her.

"I shall dress at once and go and see him. I do

not ask you to accompany me ; I shall go alone. I do not ask you to sympathise with him, but I hope, Edward, that you will not object to my doing so. I have known him ever since he was a boy ; we have grown up together ; he is the only one of my family who does not repudiate me ; he is now abandoned by all ; shall I also turn away from him, because he has committed a foolish action ? No, Edward, you would not expect me to do so. It never does harm to help persons in distress."

She said this in a very quiet and deliberate manner as if she had quite made up her mind to visit her cousin, and that nothing in the world could possibly change it. Count Klinkenstein felt enervated by the sleepless night he had passed, and as he hated a scene at any time, and especially on such occasions when he did not feel quite up to the mark, he made the entry of Lolo's maid an excuse for leaving the room, which he did, slamming the door behind him, and muttering something to himself about the intolerable eccentricities of women, and that, as far as he was concerned, Lolo might do as she pleased. He then summoned a servant, and ordered breakfast to be brought, and as he drank his coffee he grumbled to himself all the while over the worries to which a man who owned a mistress was exposed. He had nearly finished when Lolo entered the room, ready dressed to go out. She poured herself out a cup of coffee, and then bade the servant call a cab. She had not spoken a word to him or he to her, and in the nervous state in which he was he began to feel that this silence was too oppressive.

"How long will you be visiting your criminal?"
he asked her, rather surlily.

To his great surprise she went up to him, and seating herself on his knees, threw her arms round his
neck, saying : " Edward, why do you call him by that
name ? You know it is disagreeable to me. I do not
ask you to interest yourself in him ; therefore don't
you think it would be as well if we avoided talking
about him when we are together ? Let me do what I
think is right. Do not let us quarrel ; it is so easy
to do so, and what comes of it ? One never feels the
same after as before. Is it not better for us, Edward,
to continue to be friends ? "

She gave him a kiss, and he, unable to refuse anything to the pretty girl in his arms, gave her another,
and so they continued kissing till the servant returned
and announced that the cab was waiting at the door.

They parted the best of friends, and Lolo drove
away in search of her imprisoned cousin.

"After all, what does it matter if she goes and
visits her cousin ? " said the Count to himself ; " he
is a human creature, and it is an admirable trait
in woman's nature to pity misfortune and to bring
consolation to the afflicted. Men cannot blame me
because she has an idiot of a cousin who has turned
socialist ; I am not his keeper ; I have nothing to do
with him ; I am not even supposed to know him ; I
am not answerable for his education ; if it has been
bad let them lay the blame on his father. Moreover,
no man is held responsible for the vagaries of his
mistress."

He shrugged his shoulders, put on his officer's cap,

and went out to take a stroll, which he thought might soothe his irritated nerves.

Lolo drove to several prisons before she discovered the one in which her cousin was locked up. The officials who received her declined absolutely to let her see him without an order to that effect from the Prefect of Police. All her coaxing was of no avail ; the stern officials remained calm and unmoved by all her feminine wiles, so Lolo was compelled to re-enter her cab and to drive in search of that high official. She was shown into a waiting-room where she remained for more than an hour ; but she was not to be baffled. At last she was ushered in.

The Prefect received her very civilly, but he turned a deaf ear to her request ; no relatives would be allowed to visit the prisoners until after the preliminary inquiry had been held ; at the same time the great police potentate expressed his surprise that a pretty woman should take an interest in so great a criminal, and he alarmed poor Lolo by telling her that her cousin would in all probability receive a very heavy sentence, as the Government were determined to suppress socialism, which had become a great deal too rampant of late.

Lolo retired with heart very low, and drove at once to a lawyer of great reputation with the intention of engaging him for the defence. There she was again kept waiting a long while before she was able to see him. She told him her errand, and he promised to consider the case of her cousin favourably, and to let her know in a few days whether he could undertake his defence ; he was a man still young in appearance,

and the prospect of repeated visits from the pretty
Olga Zanelli, of whose fame he had heard, was more
likely to influence his decision than the question of
the righteousness of the case. He cheered her a little
by remarking that her cousin's youth would be a point
in his favour, and he was full of little attentions to
her. Then they came to business. He told her that
to defend Heinrich Lazarus efficiently would cost a
considerable sum, for political trials generally lasted
a long time. Lolo replied that the money would be
found. So they parted, and the lawyer promised to
let her know as soon as possible if he could find time
to undertake the case, and to do his best to give her
a favourable reply.

Lolo returned home late, and tired out by her unsuccessful efforts to see her troublesome cousin. The
important question, which now occupied her mind,
was how to find the necessary funds. The lawyer had
said that the proceedings might be protracted, and
the longer they were so the more expensive would be
the legal costs. The money must be found ; she
would never allow Heinrich to be sacrificed for want
of it. Count Klinkenstein had never as yet refused
her anything, but the idea of applying to him for the
money did not please her. Without being ungenerous
he might very well refuse, for what was Heinrich
Lazarus to him? and if he acceded to her wish he
would only do so after a great deal of grumbling.
No ; she preferred to make sacrifices, and to raise the
money herself. She had jewels ; she would sell as
many as were necessary. She went into her bedroom
and brought out her jewel case. It required a great

effort to think of parting with such precious things, for jewels are nearer to a woman's heart than almost anything else in this world, especially when pleasant recollections are associated with their acquisition.

Lolo laid out all her treasures on the table before her, and spent several hours in cleaning the jewels and recalling every incident connected with them, from the first and inexpensive ring the Count had presented her with in the first days of their acquaintance to the last and costly trinket he had bought for her but a few months before when they were in Paris together. They looked so pretty and fascinating lying on the table, and they were all so dear to her, that Lolo was in great perplexity to decide with which one of them she should part. Then she remembered that the lawyer had said that a great deal of money would be required, so with many pangs she finally selected her beautiful diamond necklace which Count Klinkenstein had given her a few days after she had become his mistress in the very hey-day of their first love. The sparkling gems received many a kiss, and not a few tears were shed on them before they were replaced in their velvet case and set aside to be sent to a jeweller for sale.

A few days later a large sum of money was paid to Lolo by a leading jeweller of Berlin, in whose shop window her famous necklace could now be seen exposed for sale. "Heinrich will be properly defended," she said to herself with glee, as she sat on the floor counting over what seemed to her an endless array of gold pieces. While she was thus employed she received a letter from the lawyer, informing her that he would undertake the defence of her cousin. Her joy was now complete, if, under the circumstances, she could really be said to feel any.

As Count Klinkenstein was walking away from Lolo's house he met Sydney Gray, whom he had not seen for some time, and invited him to meet him that evening in a quiet restaurant where they might dine together unobserved, and talk over various matters.

"People are talking a great deal about the arrest of a gang of socialists last night," said Sydney Gray over his soup. "The police seem to have made a rather important catch."

"They are a confounded nuisance, these socialists," answered the Count, quickly draining a tumbler full of wine.

"This spread of socialism throughout Germany is undoubtedly a very serious thing for the Government," continued the Englishman; "if the uneducated masses alone professed revolutionary ideas there would be nothing to wonder at; they do so, more or less, all over the world. Unfortunately the secret society which was pounced upon last night seems to consist, according to what I see in the evening papers, of young students and persons of education, who ought certainly to have known better than to plot foolish demonstrations."

"What do the papers say?" inquired the Count, with alacrity; "have they already found out everything about these blackguards? What a pity it is that Prince Bismarck does not put an end to the daily papers; every one would be better if they did not exist; they do nothing but propagate scandal, and draw attention to all the vices of the town, and they are inclined to make heroes of revolutionists and cutthroats, and to hold them up for the admiration of an ignorant and debauched public. Gray, what paper have you got hold of there?"

"The *Börsen Courier*, my dear Klinkenstein."

"What does it say?"

"It seems that one of the principal prisoners is the son of a court chaplain."

"Do they give his name?" asked the Count, very much annoyed and turning red.

"Heinrich something or other," replied Sydney Gray, turning over the leaves of the newspaper to find the place. "Heinrich Lazarus."

"The very man!" exclaimed the Count.

"Do you know him?" inquired Sydney Gray, rather astonished at the Count's manner.

"I wish the deuce I did not; I would give a good deal to know that that creature was at the bottom of the sea. Gray, read to me what they say about him. I suppose it is very disagreeable?"

Sydney Gray did as he was told. The passage contained several sarcastic allusions to Court Chaplain Lazarus, whose moral and Christian teaching was made answerable for his son's vagaries. It was also stated that the prisoner was a cousin of the mistress of a well-known officer of the Gardes du Corps.

"Curse the blasted Jews who own that scandal-loving commercial sheet!" shouted the Count, tearing the paper out of Gray's hands and crumpling it up with fury. "Why can these alien money-grabbers not mind their own dirty commerce, and leave gentlemen and their private affairs in peace?"

"What on earth has happened to you, Klinken-stein?"

"The matter is that the infamous creature Heinrich Lazarus is Lolo's cousin. Do you understand now? I expect the next thing that scoundrelly *Börsen Courier* will say is that I have supplied these socialists with money to help their propaganda. It would be enough to make a Prussian officer die of shame to have such a thing said of him."

"No one would believe it."

"There are always idiots enough in the world to believe any foolish and improbable story about you, especially when it does not rebound to your credit."

They remained silent for a little time, then Sydney Gray remarked,—

"By the way, Klinkenstein, how is Olga Zanelli getting on? I have not seen her since you came back from Paris."

"Oh! she is right enough as far as I know," answered the Count, affecting an air of indifference, which he thought was the proper thing for an officer to do when talking of his mistress. "Gray, why don't you go and see her more often? I know she likes you, and I should much prefer that you visited her often than my lecherous brother officers; their one idea in going to her house is to try and win her affections. As for that crowd of Bohemian scoundrels who frequent her house, actors, musicians, opera singers, artists, God knows who, I am sick of them, and one of these days I will chuck the whole lot out."

"Olga Zanelli is very pretty and fascinating," remarked Sydney Gray, with a smile; "no wonder

that men run after her with evil intentions. I suppose,
Klinkenstein, you have never run after the mistresses
of your brother officers ? "

" Never ! " replied the Count emphatically, bringing
down his fist upon the table. " Since I have known
Lolo I have been faithful to her, and no man can say
I have not."

" It is very creditable to you, Klinkenstein ; but
have you never during the time you have been with
her felt at moments tired of her society ? "

" No, certainly not."

" You have never regretted your lost freedom,
Klinkenstein, or felt at times that you had done a
foolish thing in burdening yourself with a girl of low
extraction, to whom it is impossible for you ever to
be married ? "

" I do not think I have," said the Count, not without some hesitation ; " as for her low extraction, which
you so delicately allude to, I do not mind it in the least.
She is a beautiful piece of female flesh ; her education
is quite as good as that of most girls in society, and
she is much more interesting than they are, at least
so I think ; and then we have been in love with each
other, which is a point you always forget when you
run her down in talking to me."

" My dear Klinkenstein, you are quite mistaken if
you think I have a poor opinion of your mistress ; on
the contrary, I think so highly of her that I am sorry
to see her in the position of a mistress and not of a
wife. Had you left her alone she would probably
have married some one in her own position in life
and been happy ; unfortunately you came between and

made her your mistress. How long she will remain so no one can tell ; anyhow, you have spoiled her chance of getting respectably married, and she will now probably end her days in a corrupt society, to which honest women do not belong."

"Why must you always look at the black side of things, Gray? Why must you always assume that I am incapable of constancy, and must sooner or later get tired of her?"

"I can hardly be accused of pessimism," replied Sydney Gray, "simply because I try to see things as they are, and not as I should like them to be. I do not mean to say that it is impossible for you to remain attached to Olga Zanelli to the end of your days, but I do maintain that it is highly improbable. Ardent passions are apt to cool ; young men like yourself usually believe that they will love their mistresses for ever, but when they have lived two or three years with them they begin to discover with astonishment that, however beautiful they may be, they no longer excite them to the same degree that they formerly did ; then they blame the woman as if it were her fault, and they go in search of a new girl who will restore zest to jaded appetites."

"That may be true of other people's mistresses, but it is not so of Lolo. I am as fond of her now as ever I was."

"Then I am sorry for you."

"Why?"

"Because a man should love his wife, and not his mistress."

"But if a mistress be as good as a wife?"

"In that case the man must be a fool, and his friends ought to intervene to save him."

"Would you wish me to give up Lolo?"

"Certainly, and the sooner you do so the better."

"And you want me to get married?"

"Yes," replied Sydney Gray.

Count Klinkenstein shrugged his shoulders and murmured: "Poor Lolo, every one is working to make her unhappy." Then he changed the subject of conversation.

That night as Count Klinkenstein lay sleepless in bed, he pondered over the reasons which made his many friends advise him to break with his mistress. Did they see clearer than himself? Was his connection with Lolo doing him harm, and would he be happier if he threw her over and married his cousin Nelly? It was the first time that he had allowed his mind to dwell on the possibility of his having some day to break with his mistress, and he was angry with himself for entertaining such an idea even for a moment.

END OF VOL. II.